"I'm not really y____
I'm nothing to you."

Kate's voice was tearful as she faced him.

"Oh, yes, you are," Diego ground out. "You're a daily irritation, a fiery opponent I could do without. You are prickly and domineering, with a tongue like a knife. Your stupidity is boundless—and my own must be similar, or I'd never have manoeuvred you into staying here."

Kate cringed—his anger and his words hurt. New tears flooded her eyes.

"Are you now using your feminine wiles?" he murmured, his fingers easing their grip. "You look at me with those soul-stirring blue eyes and stand crushed and defeated. Am I supposed to feel pity?"

"I'm never crushed," Kate said in a tremulous voice, "and I don't suppose you ever feel anything."

"You suppose wrongly," he said, pulling her closer before catching her lips in a deep, probing kiss.

PATRICIA WILSON used to live in Yorkshire, England, but with her children all grown-up, she decided to give up her teaching position there and accompany her husband on an extended trip to Spain. Their travels are providing her with plenty of inspiration for her romance writing.

Books by Patricia Wilson

HARLEQUIN PRESENTS

1221—THE GATHERING DARKNESS
1238—TEMPORARY BRIDE
1262—GUARDIAN ANGEL
1286—DANGEROUS OBSESSION
1310—A SECRET UNDERSTANDING
1398—PASSIONATE ENEMY

HARLEQUIN ROMANCE

2856—BRIDE OF DIAZ
3102—BOND OF DESTINY

Don't miss any of our special offers. Write to us at the following address for information on our newest releases.

Harlequin Reader Service
P.O. Box 1397, Buffalo, NY 14240
Canadian address: P.O. Box 603,
Fort Erie, Ont. L2A 5X3

PATRICIA WILSON

stormy surrender

Harlequin Books

TORONTO • NEW YORK • LONDON
AMSTERDAM • PARIS • SYDNEY • HAMBURG
STOCKHOLM • ATHENS • TOKYO • MILAN

Harlequin Presents first edition January 1992
ISBN 0-373-11430-3

Original hardcover edition published in 1990
by Mills & Boon Limited

STORMY SURRENDER

CHAPTER ONE

THERE was a man watching her, and Kate knew he had
been there for some time. The knowledge had even penetrated her misery. She could vaguely see him out of the
corner of her eye, but she didn't bother to look round
properly. There was no danger in being here alone, although the churchyard was silent and deserted. London
hummed busily beyond the high wall, its unsleeping
murmur invading even the tranquillity here on a bitterly
cold February afternoon.

The sun was weak today, but at least it shone, its cold
light touching her astonishing hair, making the red-gold
curls glitter like autumn fire. Her skin was pale and
smooth as magnolia blossom, her deep blue eyes almost
closed.

She shivered suddenly in the sharp sting of the wind
and drew her coat more closely round her slender body,
putting up the collar, tossing her long hair back and free
of it.

It wasn't just the wind. She was cold inside, deeply
cold, her normal enthusiasm for life dimmed. She would
never see them again. Both of them were gone—gone
within months of each other. They would have been
glad—they had always adored each other—but the great
dull gap that yawned before her seemed bottomless, never
to be closed.

Kate looked down at the headstone, the words
swimming before eyes that could weep no more, the tears
spent freely.

'In memory of John Hart who died September 17th...'
Her eyes blurred and fell to the other name. 'Also his
beloved wife Lucia, January 22nd...'

How long ago it seemed, but it was merely weeks since
her mother's dark eyes had closed for the last time. She
sighed and turned away, an empty glaze over the rich,
deep blue of her own eyes as she walked to the gate,
ignoring the man who watched her, too weighed down
with grief and loneliness to care who he was or why he
was there.

Irritation moved like a shadow across his dark face.
He was a foreigner. Something about the haughty ele-
gance of his stance, the total blackness of his hair, the
glitter of his eyes proclaimed a man impatient with the
cold of an English February afternoon. The impatience
and a growing anger raced across his black eyes.

She intended to ignore him. He had resolutely waited
and watched, having just missed her at the house by mere
seconds, and he did not plan to wait longer in this cold,
dismal place with the wind like a sharp dagger 'Señorita
Hart!'

The commanding tone of his voice gained her im-
mediate attention, her eyes focusing on him reluctantly.
The wind blew her glorious, tumbled hair, hair that
curled from the crown and fell in wonderful disarray to
her shoulders, and the slim hand pushed it back
carelessly.

'What do you want?' Her eyes hardly saw him at all,
but her mind noted the cold tone, the hard inflection,
and instinctively she resented him.

'Would it not be better to first enquire who I am?'

'I'm not at all sure that I care.'

Instantly he hardened further, a tempestuous flare of
anger in the night-black eyes. His gaze was so intense

on the pale oval of her face that she shuddered, slight colour flooding her skin as the reality of her rudeness put her at a disadvantage.

He was deeply tanned, his hair black as jet, heavy and thick. It did not, however, gleam as much as the black eyes that regarded her with a tightly held-in annoyance. He seemed to have been sculptured in bronze, a coldly handsome face lifted arrogantly. His clothes were elegantly perfect, a heavy and expensive sheepskin jacket open over a dark suit, and his appearance momentarily brought her to life. There was something about him that stirred lost memories, and she looked at him more closely, a flicker of alarm at the back of her mind.

'I'm sorry. I'm not normally rude. I'm afraid I resented your intrusion.'

'I did not intrude, *señorita*. I waited until your vigil was at an end.'

'My vigil?' The deep blue eyes regarded him rather vaguely and she nodded. 'Yes. I suppose you could call it that.' She took a deep, shuddering breath. 'You wish to speak to me?'

'I do. I have come to take you to Spain, to escort you to your grandmother.' He spoke sharply—in Spanish—and the flicker of alarm in Kate's mind gave place to a wave of anger.

Diego Alvarez! She must really be deeply in shock not to have placed him. It had been a long time ago, almost eight years, but he hadn't changed that much—at any rate, the commanding arrogance was still there, the haughty disapproval.

'I don't have a grandmother, *señor*.' She answered in the same language almost without thought, the deep blue eyes as cold as his.

He smiled then with tight satisfaction.

'Oh, yes, you do, *señorita*—at least, *she* insists that you do. For myself it is a matter of supreme indifference, but Doña Elvira is my grandmother too. Indulging her is, one may say, my hobby. You have changed little—your hair is still as unmistakable as a beacon in the night, you speak Spanish as fluently as ever. You may be grown up now, but you are Lucia's daughter. You will accompany me to Spain. I have come to take you home to your grandmother.'

Kate was stung into life, more life than she had felt for weeks.

'Perhaps we had better speak in English, Señor Alvarez,' she said with some asperity, giving up any idea of pretending not to recognise him. 'Obviously I'm not as fluent in your language as I believed. I will repeat my sentence carefully. I do not have a grandmother.'

She said the words slowly, each one spaced out, and his lips twitched sardonically.

'I am perfectly comfortable in either language, Señorita Hart, as you may remember, and you are Lucia's daughter whether it is stated in Spanish or English. You therefore have a grandmother—a Spanish grandmother—and I intend that she shall see you without any delay.'

'You have my permission to get lost!' she blazed, his arrogance infuriating her.

'That is no way to speak to your—cousin by adoption.'

'Adoption makes you no cousin at all, and relieves me of the responsibility of a grandmother,' Kate snapped, turning to leave.

She did not get far; in fact, she got nowhere at all. A hand like steel came to her arm, biting into her even through the heavy coat she wore.

'That is enough!' His momentary amusement died so quickly that it might never have been there at all. 'I have waited in the freezing cold for you, explained why I am here, and now the matter is ended.'

'I couldn't agree more!' Kate stopped abruptly as she became aware that a couple of interested spectators were standing quite close by, no doubt expecting a fight, although she didn't fancy her chances against this man. Normally she dispatched men with ease, her tongue a sharp weapon, her slender height putting them at a decided disadvantage, but Diego Alvarez towered over her, the advantage all his. No, he hadn't changed at all.

'Come to the house,' she hissed angrily. 'We'll shout at each other there!'

It never occurred to her to be worried about inviting him to her parents' house, although it was now bleakly empty of life. If he was crazed at all it was obviously with power. He wouldn't use physical violence to obtain obedience. She remembered that his character alone was all that was necessary. When she was seventeen he had fascinated her and frightened her too. He strode along beside her like a great, dark cat—not at all domesticated, but she was not now seventeen. Things had changed and so had she.

If it were possible to have a village within a city, then this was it. Her father had been a doctor here for most of his married life and her mother had been well liked. People greeted her quietly as she strode along, their voices sympathetic, their eyes questioningly on the tall dark stranger whose pace was adjusted to match hers.

She could feel anger seething from him, and it did nothing to reduce her own annoyance. She didn't want a domineering male around. She was still numb and shocked by her loss. He was forcing her away from the grief she clung to because there was nothing else to cling to, and she resented him more bitterly than ever. Just who did he think he was, coming here right out of the blue and treating her as if she were still a child?

Kate walked up the short flight of steps to the front door of her parents' house. She hadn't even looked at him as they walked along, and he had ignored her too, making no attempt to placate her, although he was very well aware that she was extremely annoyed. She flung the door open, stepping aside as he followed, and the icy cold of the house hit them immediately, taking even her by surprise. She had not been in here since the funeral and the house had not been heated for weeks.

'*Dios!* It is small wonder that you are pale as a lily!' He glared at her as if she had deliberately invited him in to freeze, and she bridled anew.

'The heating is off, Señor Alvarez,' she snapped. 'I don't live here. This was my parents' house—my old home. I have a flat in Central London.'

'It must be expensive,' he mused balefully, the black eyebrows drawn together in a disapproving scowl. His eyes moved to the red Audi Quattro parked by the steps. 'Yours, *señorita*?'

'Mine! Earned the hard way, *señor*. I have a very responsible and well-paid job in the City.' She turned away, two bright spots of colour on her high cheekbones. What the hell did he think she did for a living? And, whatever he thought, what gave him the right to question her? They had barely exchanged a dozen sentences. It was years since she had known him, but he was taking her to task as if he were her keeper.

'I'll put on the heating and then we can settle down to raging,' she offered sarcastically.

'It would be better perhaps to leave here at once and go to your flat. It will be some while before the heating takes effect and you have yet to pack your things. I do not have time to stay in England. I have a great deal of work waiting for me in Spain.'

'I agree. It would be better to leave. The house is to be sold, but not for a few months. There's no reason for me to be here at the moment.' She spun round to march back to the door and he followed, waiting as she locked up, cool satisfaction on his face. She remembered that he was quite accustomed to being obeyed. This was where his cold arrogance could take a tumble.

Surreptitiously she glanced down the street. This was a quiet cul-de-sac and she needed only to look one way. There was no sign of a Rolls-Royce, a Mercedes, Porsche or any other vehicle worthy of Diego Alvarez. Her lips tightened grimly and she walked to her car, unlocking it and getting quickly inside, lowering the window as the engine came smoothly to powerful life.

'Goodbye, *señor*!' She turned her fiery head and glared into his angry eyes. 'Give my regards to your grandmother and tell her that I don't need any relatives at all!'

She spun the fast car in a tight circle and roared away, too intent on the road at this speed to have time to glance back, her hands shaking on the wheel. She had never met anyone who riled her so much. The feeling was so painfully strong that she took no joy in her victory. She just wanted to put a lot of distance between them, because those black, flashing eyes seemed to be burned into her mind.

He had intruded on her grief and behaved as if she had nothing to grieve about at all. He was a man with no gentleness, a stranger from long ago who had expected her to listen like a simpleton and follow him to Spain.

How dared he? She tightened her mouth and frowned at the road. He had spoiled her last day of solitude, and she felt guilty that she could no longer concentrate on her parents. The dark, cold face seemed to have blotted every other thought from her head.

The next day found Kate back at work, her long compassionate leave over, and she was glad to feel the familiar atmosphere close around her. Merrol and Jones was a prestigious firm of interior designers and decorators catering solely for the very wealthy, and Kate was the star of the firm.

'You're back, Kate.' Felix Merrol came up behind her quietly, taking her arm and leading her to his office. Inside he shut the door and looked at her closely. 'You look a bit better. The other day when I called at the flat to see you I very nearly refused to go. You looked ill with misery. I'm glad you're coming out of it.'

She hadn't been—not until yesterday. It was that irritating, uncompromising Spaniard. Antagonism had boosted her out of her grief to a certain extent. It had given her something to think about, and she had spent the previous evening seething with rage and resentment.

'I was involved in a fight,' she informed Felix drily. 'It gave me something to concentrate on besides self-pity.'

His lips quirked. 'You don't look damaged, so you must have won as usual, and you never have been given to self-pity. Tell me about the fight.'

'I'll tell you later.' Kate suddenly didn't want to speak about Diego Alvarez. Felix would hoot with laughter and it wasn't at all funny. It had been very unsettling, past embarrassment and present misery all combined with rage.

'A drink after work?' he enquired hopefully, and this time she said yes. She wanted to get back to work, back to her drawing-board. Besides, he had made the thought of that hateful man rear up once again to the top of her mind.

She had to tell him later, though, as they had a drink in a nearby wine bar, and as she had expected he almost collapsed with laughter.

'You should have gone, Kate,' he grinned, after she had stared at him in annoyance and he had got himself under control. 'We've been trying to get a foothold in Spain for years. All that lovely property, all those grand old mansions, the castles...' He waved his hand extravagantly. 'Do you know the place?'

'I used to, and, in any case, I've heard about it all my life. It's called the Monastery of the Eagles. It's perched between the mountains and the sea in the south-east of Spain and it's very beautiful. My mother missed it always.'

'She never went back?'

'Not until I was seveteen. There was a family row initially, and the return wasn't a raging success.' Kate shrugged. 'It was all over a long time ago. Going back was a mistake and it did nothing to make Mother happy. It was the one and only time that I went to Spain—once too often!'

'But I thought you spoke Spanish fluently.'

'I do, but only because my mother was a Spaniard. Anyway,' she added, determinedly drawing the conversation to an end, 'I don't have a grandmother and I'm not going, so that's that!'

'Did I even suggest it?' Felix asked in pained surprise. 'I want you here where I can see you.'

She laughed then, and looked up at him, her deep blue eyes mocking. 'If I ever say yes one of these times when you ask me to marry you, you'll run a mile.'

'Try me!' Felix said sternly, a flare of laughter at the back of his eyes.

'Let's wait until we're more mature,' Kate suggested with a grin.

He drove her back to her flat. Today she hadn't brought her car, and now that the time had come she shrank from the idea of the Underground.

He looked hopeful as he got out to open her door, but she shook her head and neatly took her keys from his hand.

'I'm not inviting you in, Felix. You'll talk at me for hours.'

'Would I do such a thing? If I did it would all be praise. I called round at Belton last night. It's really something, they're delighted. It cost them a packet too. You're brilliant, Kate.'

'Well, then,' Kate soothed, and he grinned into her upturned face.

'You know I'm in love with you?'

'I know. Next to you—I'm the one. Goodnight, Felix. You're a very unusual boss, and I enjoyed doing Belton Castle, by the way. Praise is always acceptable, though.'

'Give mi a chance, luv,' he begged in a voice filled with coarse-theatrical passion. He aimed a juicy kiss at her, which she couldn't quite dodge as she made a laughing escape into the flat.

Thank heaven for Felix. He could lift her out of misery. She should have gone back to work sooner. As for marrying him, it was a game he played. The thought would frighten him to death. He was definitely a bachelor born and bred. The idea of opposing him in the kitchen was enough to bring a shudder to any woman who knew him. He carried his artistic ability right through to the soufflé.

She took off her coat and turned to her own kitchen, surprised and then amused as the doorbell rang. She knew who it was—Felix with another gag—and her face was wreathed in smiles as she went to open the door for him.

'Felix!' she began warningly, but her amusement faded into stunned surprise as her eyes fell, not on the fair skin and blond hair of her boss, but on the darkly chiselled, dynamic face of Diego Alvarez.

She just stared at him, and the dark brows drew together over glittering eyes. He looked almost demonic, standing there in the darkness, and it slowly sank in that he was furiously angry, his lean, athletic body holding in a rage that threatened to escape and kill her. She stepped back involuntarily and he entered without a word, his menacing gaze never leaving her, his power subduing her without one word being spoken.

He slammed the door behind him, his lips in one straight, angry line.

'I suggest that we begin again, Señorita Hart,' he grated. 'I will begin first. I have come to take you to your grandmother!'

'I've been thinking about you,' Kate informed him through lips that threatened to shake, 'and I've come to the conclusion that you're mad.'

'Your conclusions do not interest me, *señorita*!' he rasped, taking her arm in a tight grip and staring into the deep blue eyes that couldn't manage to look away. 'I am merely concerned with getting you to Spain and handing you over to your grandmother.'

'I'm not a parcel!' Kate stormed, getting her fight back and trying to pull free. 'Let go of me! You have no right to either be in my flat or touch me at all.'

'It is not my intention to be eluded again.' He tightened his grip and led her into her own sitting-room as if he owned the place. 'We are now in your flat, where presumably you have your belongings. Pack them! When your lover returns he will find you gone.'

She stared at him puzzled and outraged. Lover? It suddenly dawned on her that he meant Felix. This impossible Spaniard with the unforgiving eyes must have been lurking about outside when Felix brought her home. He had obviously seen their rather extravagant parting. She decided not to disillusion him.

'We're in London, Señor Alvarez,' she reminded him coldly. 'I have no intention of going anywhere, and the sooner you realise that, the sooner you'll be able to get back to all that work waiting for you in Spain. I work in London and I'm not leaving.'

He let her go, but he did not step back from her. Instead, his eyes moved over the pale beauty of her angry face.

'Doña Elvira is a very old lady, you must know that,' he said quietly. 'She cannot live for a great deal longer.'

'My mother isn't alive at all,' Kate said bitterly. 'She didn't manage to be an old lady. Don't change your tactics, Señor Alvarez. I've used up my tears. I just haven't any left to spare for an old lady who was content to see my mother leave, an old lady who never tried to find her and who didn't take it too well when my mother went back.'

'Eighteen years later! In any case, she was unable to find Lucia.'

'But she's found me now, when it seems to suit her, hasn't she?' Kate's blue eyes flashed at him scathingly, and his perfect lips twisted ruefully, his expression a little softened.

'I found you, *señorita*. Lucia helped me, though, otherwise I would not have been able to.' His hand went to his pocket, bringing out a letter, and even before he handed it to her Kate recognised her mother's writing. 'Before she died, Lucia wrote to my grandmother. She wrote for forgiveness. She also wished *Abuela* to know you better. I am here not only because my grandmother expects it but because Lucia wished it. Your mother wanted you to go to Spain and join your family. We are fully aware that you now have no family but us.'

'I don't need a family at all,' Kate said tremulously, the grief she had fought away beginning to flood back at the sight of her mother's handwriting. 'Everything I have, everything I do, is here in London.'

'Read the letter,' he insisted quietly, his eyes on her trembling lips. 'I do not expect you to take my word, and I almost understand your reluctance, although I must admit that I had not expected you to be so wildly antagonistic. Still,' he added with a resigned sigh, 'you are Lucia's daughter and you have changed little.'

'What is that supposed to mean?'

Her bright, glossy head shot up, her blue eyes deep and prepared to battle. He was not rising to the bait this time, though. His black brows rose quizzically. 'Are you always like this?' he enquired mildly. 'My remarks could be taken as complimentary. Lucia was a Spaniard, and Spanish woman are prepared to fight for the man they want. Clearly you do not wish to be separated from this lover. I understand.'

'You understand nothing whatsoever!' Kate snapped, a little tired of having Felix foisted on her as a lover, any amusement in that direction now quite gone and a few unwanted memories sneaking into her head. 'You've come here with every intention of getting your own way and——'

'Read the letter, *señorita*,' he suggested sardonically. 'Let us work from a basis of fact. As to getting my own way, I usually do, if you remember. I also am a Spaniard.'

'How did you find me here?' she demanded angrily, standing stiffly in front of him with no intention of giving way at all. 'The letter would be from my old home.'

'People in England are not at all kind in my opinion,' he murmured coolly. 'They do, however, have what I believe you call a soft spot for poor foreigners who speak very little of their language. A few stumbling words of English and they are prepared to tell you anything at all.'

'You speak fluent English!' Kate snapped, her face outraged.

'Only when I need to, *señorita*,' he assured her mockingly. 'Now let us get down to important things.'

He held out the letter and Kate snatched it from him, glaring at him, and then turning away to sit down and read. He stood watching her until she invited him to sit down, her voice too filled with hostility to be at all gracious.

Her mother's writing swam before her eyes for a moment before she could begin to read. Señora Elvira Alvarez was the woman who had adopted her mother when she was a child, the woman Diego Alvarez called grandmother.

Kate knew the story. Her mother had run away to England and Kate had thought it wonderfully romantic, but, as the years had passed and she had begun to realise just what isolation from her family and her country meant to her mother, she had come to resent them bitterly. They had loved Lucia enough to adopt her, but obviously they were coldly aristocratic and had never forgiven the way she had left. That was not love, in Kate's opinion. Love forgave. She had grown up thinking the Alvarez family too stiff-necked and proper to feel anything other than pride, and a brief trip there with her mother had confirmed it.

As she read the letter, though, Kate knew that there was more than that to the story. Her mother's feeling of guilt breathed from the pages. She assured Señora Alvarez that she regretted her foolishness, she called her *madrecita* and mourned the fact that their reunion had not been too happy. She begged her to really get to know the granddaughter she had seen so briefly.

Diego Alvarez had been speaking the truth, but Kate was left feeling puzzled. There was something else. Every instinct told her that. Things went deeper.

'I believe you,' she said quietly, glancing up at him, the anger fading away in spite of the look of power and arrogance that covered him like a cloak, 'but there's more to it than this, isn't there?'

He looked at her for a few disquieting seconds and then leaned back in his chair, facing her. 'You do not know, do you? Did your mother become so like the English that every bit of passion left her?' His eyes moved over her face and his lips twitched in amusement. 'Perhaps not. There is certainly a fire in you, even though it is used as a weapon. There was fire in you at seventeen. Lucia left Spain in a rage, threatening self-destruction. She brought turmoil to the *monasterio* and to her mother. She also came very close to ruining my father's life, in which case I would never have been born. I would have resented that,' he finished, with a derisive look at her.

'My mother was gentle and kind——'

'Because she obviously found the right man,' he interrupted. 'She was lucky. At one time she was obsessively devoted to my father. She expected marriage and behaved like a tornado when she discovered that my father was already in love—with my mother.'

'She was quiet—peaceful . . . I can't believe . . .'

'You must believe, *señorita*, because you will be living in the same house as my mother, and no doubt she will be wary of Lucia's daughter now that you are a woman. One tornado in a lifetime is sufficient.'

'Y-your father . . .' Kate began. 'But they must have been brought up as brother and sister.'

'But well aware that they were not related,' he finished. 'Theoretically you are my cousin; actually we are not in any way related. Gerardo, my father, became her obsession, the man she imagined she loved.' His lips twisted with irony. 'Love is, after all, mainly a matter of imagination.'

'Not for my mother and father!' Kate snapped. 'They were devoted to each other and died within months of each other. She couldn't bear to live without him.' Tears came to her eyes, but she blinked them away angrily. 'What has all this to do with me?'

'Lucia at last repented,' he reminded her coldly. 'She is dead and unable to give any comfort to my grandmother. You will do that, *señorita*. You will come to Spain and restore an old lady's faith in her own judgement. She has clung determinedly to her love for Lucia. You will repay that faith.'

'She didn't seem to have much love for my mother when we came to Spain——'

'You were merely a child and too involved with your own daydreams to notice.' The cool voice slashed at her, and Kate sprang up to pace about restlessly, too embarrassed suddenly to tell him to go and comfort his grandmother himself. *His* grandmother? Her mother had stated in her letter in no uncertain terms that she was her own grandmother also. Kate was too confused to think straight, and at that moment she felt little older than the girl who had been in awe of Diego Alvarez so long ago. He did not, however, manage to make her feel small and above her station in life. That kind of thing was long past.

'I'll make you some coffee,' she muttered, escaping to the kitchen, and clearly he knew she had to come to terms with things to some extent, because he said nothing and let her go.

She caught sight of herself in the full-length mirror in the hall. She didn't seem to have one ounce of Spanish blood in her—her features, her skin, her colouring were all from her father. For some reason she had never looked like her mother, but it did nothing to dull the ache of love inside her. Was this what her mother wanted her to do, to atone for her own mistake?

She filled the kettle, got the cups and saucers down, and then stared into space, leaning against the cupboards. It had all come back, the emptiness, the grief. Hot tears filled her eyes and ran to her cheeks, and she was startled and embarrassed when a slight noise had her turning to see Diego Alvarez leaning against the kitchen door, watching her.

'I'm not about to escape!' she snapped, wiping frantically at her tears.

'I did not expect it,' he said quietly. 'You have not lost everyone. You have a family, even though it is not a real one. Perhaps *Abuela* will also give comfort to you.'

'I don't want comfort,' Kate muttered, turning away from the dark eyes.

'My grandmother *does*!' he snapped, the momentary gentleness fading rapidly. 'You do not have to be comforted. It is your own choice. In the matter of my grandmother's peace of mind, however, there is no choice. One way or another, you will come to Spain!'

Later, as they sat and drank coffee in silence, Kate came to a decision. She was beginning to feel guilty. She had a vivid imagination, and she could almost see the shocked grief of the old lady as her mother stormed and raged. She would never have believed it, but she had read the letter. She was left with a debt she had never imagined, but it was there and undeniable, he was right. She had a few ghosts to lay on her own account too. A brief visit and she could put the past behind her—the nearer and the more distant past.

'I'll come,' she said carefully, expecting a show of hostility, 'but I can't come now. I have a job, responsibilities of my own.'

'I have investigated your job,' he stated, his dark eyes on her strained face. 'You are their star attraction, are you not? I can understand that you must ask for leave.'

'There'll be no trouble, I expect,' she said a trifle thoughtlessly, her mind on other things, hardly taking in his words. 'Felix will let me go to Spain.'

'Felix? Ah, yes. The man you expected as I knocked. The man who brought you home. Apparently he is an indulgent lover to allow you to leave instead of keeping you firmly by his side.'

'He's my boss!' she snapped, all guilty thoughts vanishing at the return to battle. 'My employer!'

'How very convenient. It is all settled, then, as he is obviously about to refuse you nothing. When will you come?'

She stared at him vindictively, almost ready to say that she wouldn't go at all. Here was a man to infuriate to the point of making her want to attack him physically. No, he didn't frighten her any more. He couldn't embarrass her either. Narrowed dark eyes held hers though, pin-points of fire deep in his gaze, the hard, arrogant face alert.

'If we have to begin all over again, I am quite prepared to do so,' he assured her threateningly. 'I am also prepared to return should you promise to come and then break your word. I would not, however, come in any good frame of mind.'

Did he imagine he had come in a good frame of mind this time? Great Scott! He was impossible, worse than ever!

'I'll come!' she told him tightly. 'I'll come in a week, if I can get permission for more leave.' She glared at him. 'And don't threaten me, Señor Alvarez!'

'Threaten you, *señorita*? I am being particularly careful with you. You are my cousin.'

'I'm nothing at all!' she snapped, and his eyes flashed in amusement.

'Do not underestimate yourself, Kathryn,' he murmured mockingly.

'Providence,' Felix said smugly when she went in to work to tell him, 'has an unerring ability to make itself felt when least expected. Leave is granted. You may very well become my toe-hold in Spain. I expect many good things to stem from this mission of mercy.'

It was a relief that he had taken it so well. She had already had compassionate leave, and now this so soon afterwards. Luckily there were no big commissions at the moment.

'Is he hanging around waiting for you?' Felix asked innocently, looking mischievously over her shoulder, and such was her state of wariness as far as Diego Alvarez was concerned that she instantly looked anxiously behind her. 'Got you worried, hasn't he?' Felix enquired wryly.

'He's impossible,' Kate snapped, frowning at the thought of the domineering Spaniard. She wouldn't have been at all surprised to find him standing silently behind her, although she knew perfectly well he had gone back to Spain—after several suitable threats had been delivered regarding her promise to follow within one week.

'Never mind,' Felix soothed. 'Go out there, visit your grandma and bring back a lot of lovely business.'

'I haven't got a grandmother,' Kate reminded him forcefully. Neither did she have a tall, dark, arrogant cousin, but he was about as easy to dismiss as an earthquake. He had made her squirm in the past, and no doubt he was preparing to start all over again. Let him try!

CHAPTER TWO

A WEEK later Kate arrived in Spain and, at the sight of her, two porters were almost fighting for the privilege of wheeling her luggage. She was glad to hand over to the winner because she felt worried all over again. She wasn't quite sure who would meet her, but she was certain that somebody would. There was little chance of Diego Alvarez allowing her to disappear when he had her at last in Spain.

A flare of unease crossed her face. This was going to be very difficult, and not by any stretch of the imagination could she say she was looking forward to it. She had the irritated feeling that she had allowed herself to be bullied—for the first time in her life.

The memories of her stay here in her teens were still gnawing away. For years she had pushed aside that particular time, the feeling of injustice, the embarrassment. There had been a time when she'd cringed at the idea of ever meeting Diego again. Now she was here after a battle with him, and she had the distinct impression that he was still capable of looking down at her as if she were of no consequence.

He had come himself. She saw him waiting, and for a moment her heart gave an uncomfortable lurch. He had seen her first and he was watching her, standing behind the barrier, his dark eyes intent. He didn't smile, but there was a satisfaction in the eyes that studied her that told her he had half expected her to forget her promise.

It suddenly occurred to her that he seemed to be hypnotising her. Her eyes were roaming almost of their own free will over the tall perfection, the wide shoulders, the lean hips, the stunning masculine grace. Now he was in pale grey trousers and sports shirt, and he looked more striking than before. She had seen some wonderful men in her time, but she had to admit reluctantly that none of them could even remotely compare to this man. She still felt the awe she had felt at seventeen, when she had first seen him.

He stood watching her coolly, with a sardonic glance that brought colour to her face as he inspected every inch of her. His eyes flared over her, their black glitter finally resting on her face and her cascades of fiery hair, and Kate found herself taking a very uneven breath. She was eight years back, facing that scathing glance that told her she was not at all suitable to mix with the Alvarez clan. Her heart was hammering as if she had been running uphill, and her face felt hot as the dark eyes acknowledged her confusion with a slight smile.

He came forward and took charge of everything, signalling the man with the trolley to follow, his gesture imperious.

'My car is outside. If you are not too tired after your flight we will go straight to the *monasterio*.'

'I'm quite all right,' Kate said stiffly, and he glanced at her, an all-encompassing glance that saw more than she would have wished.

'There is nothing to worry about,' he assured her, his voice lowered to avoid the ears of the very interested porter. 'They are expecting you at home and you are welcome.'

'Thank you. It—it's a little alarming to be suddenly faced with ...'

'A family? My grandmother is longing to see you.'

'But you weren't,' she said, acknowledging that it was an unwise remark, but unable to stop the surge of irritation that his very casual coolness brought. And that wasn't what she had meant at all, anyway. She had been about to say 'faced with the past'—a remark that would have been more unwise still.

'I do not do much in the way of longing,' he assured her mockingly. 'None the less, I am delighted that you have arrived. I do not have time to chase you again.'

'I'm not accustomed to being chased!' Kate snapped.

'Really? You surprise me,' he murmured drily. 'For myself, I am immune to eyes like deep blue velvet and cascades of fiery hair, but I realise that others may not be equally immune.'

'I'm not a doll, Señor Alvarez!' Kate seethed. 'My work is very skilled and demanding, and I do have my fair share of intelligence.'

'Have I doubted it?' he enquired with infuriating surprise, adding sardonically, 'As to being a doll, if you were, you would certainly not be sold easily. Your tongue would guarantee that you were left sitting on the shelf. Perhaps my brother will not be quite as taken with you as he was when you were seventeen.'

She must have been more tired than she imagined, because that was when she wanted to turn and beat him, to rage at him and see his *genuine* surprise. She held her tongue—with difficulty. So he hadn't forgotten anything? He intended to bring all that up again!

She was not too startled to see a Lamborghini parked in readiness for their departure—he was too wealthy and impressive to settle for anything quiet—and she slid elegantly into the passenger seat as he stowed away her luggage and tipped the porter. He came to take the wheel, but turned to her before starting the car.

'Now, it is clear that you and I still strike sparks off each other. It is all very amusing, but there is *Abuela* to consider. In her presence it will be necessary to bury our differences and behave as family——'

'Which we are not!' Kate interrupted.

'Which we are not,' he agreed. 'Nevertheless, we will try to be civilised with each other. You may begin by calling me Diego and not *señor*. Your little charade when we met again is now over. I shall call you Kathryn.'

'If we're pretending properly,' she said tightly, 'you'd better call me Kate. Everybody else does.' He hadn't taken into account at all that she had been dazed and shocked when she first saw him. Besides, she had spent a long time pushing him out of her mind, and hadn't been able to quite believe at first that he had been there, standing in front of her.

'You may keep that for your lover. I will call you Kathryn as I did before. I see no reason to change.'

His voice was flat, disinterested, and he glanced at his watch before taking off with a great roar of power. She imagined he had said all he intended to say. She relaxed and tried to breathe slowly. Why did he upset her so much? She wasn't seventeen now. She didn't give in easily with anyone, but she normally managed to get on well with people. She would battle with Diego every day, though, until she left Spain—of that she was more than certain.

An hour later, with the road climbing and twisting alarmingly, Kate caught the occasional glitter of blue sea, the car eating up the miles as they headed into the mountains, the countryside becoming more arid with every mile. It was hot and dusty and almost impossible to imagine that this very morning she had boarded a plane to this land and left behind a countryside sprinkled with snow.

She ventured a remark as the car slowed to negotiate a difficult part. He seemed quite content to sit in silence, but the thought of the ordeal before her made her seek some kind of companionship, even if it was only from Diego.

'Hasn't it rained?'

'Very little. We have had quite a few showers, but it will rain heavily in a couple of weeks and then things will look very different. This is one of the driest and warmest parts of Spain. The mountains here are not high and snow-capped like the Sierra Nevada, but they have their own kind of beauty and we have a great advantage in the mountains—we are not beset by tourists. You will get used to the dryness. There is tranquillity.'

Kate couldn't remember a lot of that with him around, but she kept the thought to herself. She stirred uncomfortably. Maybe this had not been one of her best ideas. Maybe she should have flatly refused to come.

'I doubt if I'll be here long enough to get used to it,' she said tightly. He didn't answer, and she glanced across at him, her mind reluctantly admitting that he was both handsome and alarming, not changed at all. His silence was becoming unnerving. 'I never found out much about the *monasterio*.'

She hadn't. She had been too taken with the atmosphere that permeated everything, and finally too busy avoiding any meeting with Diego.

'There is little to tell. It has not belonged to the Church for over a hundred years. It was abandoned and almost derelict when it came into my family's possession. Over the years it has been restored and refurbished. From the outside it is still as it was, a *monasterio*. Inside, though, it is a very large and comfortable house. There is nothing to fear. No doubt you remember enough to be assured that you are not about to be housed in a cell.'

'I'm not particularly fearful,' Kate said, with an irritated glance at him. It might be a good idea if he remembered they were supposed to be trying to be civilised. It had been his idea.

'No, I cannot imagine that you would be. You were not too fearful as a young girl. Time has not altered you much.' He didn't sound particularly pleased about that, and lapsed into silence at once.

Just sitting beside him made her feel wary. Diego would make an enemy of the most powerful kind. He had made Kate and Lucia leave when they had visited the *monasterio*, wielding his power without justice. There was little, if any sign about him that could lead her to believe he would even bend slightly. There was not even a trace of gentleness. Her eyes moved to the lean brown hands that held the wheel, guiding the fast car with easy skill, and an unexpected feeling raced down her spine. For a second she had wondered what it would be like if he touched her—really touched her. Her face flushed and she looked hurriedly away, turning her head aside.

'You are nervous?' The dark voice insinuated itself into her mind and she sat upright, holding herself stiffly.

'No. I'm merely tired. It wasn't a particularly good flight.'

'We will not be long. If you look to the front instead of hiding your head so carefully you will see our destination.'

She turned, and then all other thoughts left her mind as she saw again the place her mother had called home.

In the distance she could see the higher hills that edged the mountains, two great crags dominating the landscape. The land was mellow, red and gold with the soft green of the trees around it, and perched on one crag was a building of great beauty. It was towering, awe-inspiring, the mellow rose-tinted stone seeming to be almost part of the rock-face itself. She could see it clearly, the low surrounding wall stretching to the edge of the sheer drop to the valley floor.

Across the valley, on the facing crag that was even higher, a towering figure of Christ stood with arms outstretched. It was white, probably marble, she thought, and its size was impossible to judge. It must have been about sixty feet high, and was so beautiful that Kate's breath caught in her throat as it had done when she had first seen it.

The *monasterio* and the *Cristo* towered above the countryside, the harsh outlines of mountains behind them, the sea, glittering and blue, a view that would be dazzling from those heights. She made no comment, and Diego drove on without a word until they were again climbing on twisting, narrow roads.

'It is still as beautiful, Kathryn? Yes?'

His soft tone surprised her and she answered in the same way without thinking. 'I can't remember having seen anything quite so beautiful before or since. My mother missed this place always.'

'She did not miss it enough to wish to return, to wish to make her peace with her family until eighteen years later.'

He had hardened instantly and Kate tightened up inside at this return to hostility. 'Maybe she didn't dare!' she snapped.

'Perhaps,' he conceded. 'Love, I am told, is a very debilitating thing. It saps the mind.'

'As you seem to get most of your information about it second-hand, then you'll never know, will you?' Kate threw at him crisply.

'*Espero que no,*' he jeered. 'I would not wish to be anything other than in complete control of my mind and my emotions. As you seem to have first-hand knowledge about this mythical state, you will perhaps enlighten me while you are here in Spain.'

'Perish the thought,' Kate murmured sarcastically. 'I never attempt the impossible. I'm sure your emotions have been carved out of the mountains. It would probably take a charge of dynamite to make them even rock a little.'

To her surprise he was silent, and then, just as she was getting her breath back, he laughed, a dark, amused sound that alarmed her.

'You are filled with hostility and the desire for combat. Your temper is still as fiery as your hair. Normally, I would still feel the desire to shake you and put you back on a plane with all speed. To my great astonishment, however, I like you. It must be because you are my cousin and grown up at last.'

Kate gasped at this condescending admission and turned on him swiftly. 'Please don't do me any favours!' she fumed. 'Now you've bared your soul to me, I'll return the compliment. I still find you arrogant, domineering and utterly impossible. To stay under the same roof I'll need dark glasses and cotton wool in my ears. As to being your cousin, I am no such thing. As a cousin you would be unacceptable, as a man you're——'

'Terrifying?' he suggested ironically. 'Perhaps you are letting the past colour your mind? Or is it merely because your lover is weak and indulgent? I noticed that he was very wary about kissing you, and that you did not accept it graciously.'

'People who spy on others get a very distorted view,' Kate informed him smartly. 'It's called key-hole vision.'

He threw his head back and laughed delightedly, and it silenced her as nothing else could have done. Laughter transformed him; it always had done. It made him into another person. The hard masculinity softened, and the coolly handsome face had come to vibrant life. He was a dangerous man—fascinating. Every instinct told her that, and the glittering dark glance that flashed her way confirmed it. A *frisson* of alarm raced over her skin. She still hated him. She was sure of that. She had to be sure, because he had made an enemy of himself long ago.

The car was now climbing through forests, the road slicing between the trees, a continuous sheer drop beside the car as the land fell away through thick forest dappled by sunlight. For a while it was impossible to see anything other than the beauty of the trees, but they climbed much higher, the road, high and perilous, winding around the end of the deep valley, and Kate could then see the *monasterio* all the way.

Gardens climbed the opposite side, disappearing into the trees that clothed the very edge of the crag, and great wrought-iron gates stood open to the courtyard at the entrance. The house was on three sides of this great courtyard, nestling in the sun of the late afternoon, and it was an enormous size, bigger than she remembered it, more imposing.

And suddenly they were there. The car sped along the rough track that now flattened out, and before long they were stopping in the courtyard that nestled sleepily before the great house. In the very centre a fountain played. It was large, high, surrounded by flowering bushes and small banks of flowers. White doves wandered around, flying from time to time to the high roof-tops, their soft, melodious sounds filling the air. The smell of flowers, the cascading fountain and the murmuring of the doves were almost hypnotic, and Kate came out of a sort of trance to see a servant hurrying over to them.

'Garage the car, José!' Diego ordered. 'I shall not need it again today.'

'*Sí*, Don Diego.'

The deferential tone had Kate glancing at Diego. She had been very impressed as a teenager to hear him called that, but he was used to it and merely handed the keys to José, who immediately began to unload her luggage as Kate found herself being escorted through the huge doors that led off the courtyard, Diego urging her indoors as if she were about to bolt. Her luggage, he murmured, would find its way to her room. She never doubted it; how would it dare do otherwise?

As soon as she saw the great wide hall, the ceiling, sculptured and carved with frescos disappearing into the dim heights, Kate's doubts about her visit momentarily vanished. Two staircases led from the hall and joined at the top where a gallery with carved posts looked down, coloured shields and flags hanging from it. There was nothing but artistic delight and professional approval on her face as she slowed her steps and gazed around. It was this house that had inspired her to take up her present profession. She had never forgotten it.

'I see that you still approve of my home,' Diego said quietly. 'You will find it slightly changed from the times when you wandered through it as a girl. The whole place was refurbished some time ago, all but the *sala grande*.

That was a little too spectacular and difficult for the firm who did the rest. My grandmother too was unwilling to place such difficult work in the hands of anyone other than some genius. Perhaps she will let you get your hands on it?'

He sounded sceptical, as if she were a painter and decorator, and she resisted the temptation to reel off her successes. If Felix knew about the *sala grande* he would be here post-haste to sell them the idea of her skill. She had never had the nerve to venture in there when she was seventeen. She had no desire in any case to stay close to Diego Alvarez for such a length of time, or even for any time at all.

A woman stepped out of one of the rooms and came forward to meet them, and Kate felt a wave of anxiety. She knew who it was even before Diego spoke.

'My mother, Señora Liliana Alvarez, *señorita*,' he said formally, and then smiled with unexpected amusement. 'I have captured Kathryn at last and brought her home, *madrecita*. She is not at all sure that this is a good idea, however.'

'Then we must impress her,' Liliana Alvarez said gently. 'You are a woman, Kathryn. The last time I saw you, you were a slender girl. Eight years have changed us all, but you are more beautiful than ever. Your grandmother has taken on a new lease of life at the idea of your coming, and we are all a little nervous to have such an expert in our midst. I hope you will find that the *monasterio* has been updated tastefully. Diego has told us that you are the very best in a prestigious firm.'

'From what I've already seen, it's beautiful,' Kate assured her hurriedly. She wondered what else Diego had said about her. The small amount of praise about her skills would probably have been rationed out among the list of her failings. It was such a relief to find his mother so gentle—unbelievably so at the side of her son's aggressive power. Before, Liliana Alvarez had been distant and courteous, but now Kate understood why. It must have hurt to have her mother in the house again.

'You will take Kathryn to see Doña Elvira?' his mother asked, but Diego shook his head.

'Not until I have seen *Abuela* myself. This means a lot to her, and I must first find out how she feels this afternoon. Meanwhile, I think that Kathryn is tired. It is a long and trying journey from the airport.' He indicated the contents of the heavy silver tray that had been brought in by a silent and discreet servant as they talked. 'Rest for a while and take some refreshment. I will presently go to see your grandmother.'

He didn't add, And remember to be civilised when you meet her, but it was all there in the dark, penetrating eyes and Kate felt again almost hypnotised. At any rate, the fight died in her suddenly and she sat down rather abruptly, extremely embarrassed when he came and poured her tea and handed it to her with a gesture that was all courtesy and not in any way reprimanding. It made her feel a little small, as if she had been a bad girl. And that was nothing new either. Those dark eyes had looked at her like that many times in the past.

She looked abruptly away as his eyes met hers. There was a raw sexuality about this man. She recognised that now. He was vibrantly masculine, and she wasn't even sure if he realised it. She was certain that it would be beneath his dignity. In any case, she had had enough of everything—temporarily. It was the journey, no doubt.

'You will wish to go to your room, I expect, Kathryn,' Liliana said, after a few words with Diego and having looked at their reaction to each other with some amusement. 'I will have someone show you the way.'

Kate smiled her thanks. She was beginning to get a very tight feeling inside. Not long ago she had been utterly shattered at the loss of her mother. It had left her with a great empty void inside, and only determination had pulled her through the dreadful time. Now she was back in the place where her mother had spent a great deal of her life, and her own imagination was threatening to run riot. She was seeing her mother in this room, in this household. She was also seeing herself here, unsure and impressionable.

Diego gave her a very penetrating look and then left to see his grandmother, and Kate too stood as Liliana pressed a small silver bell.

'My mother...now I know...Diego told me that——' she began, but Liliana Alvarez came quickly forward and laid her hand on Kate's arm.

'It was a long time ago,' she said softly. 'We were all very young. For a while the peace of this place was shattered, but things have a way of working out. I had many blissful years with Gerardo, and now I have my sons. Lucia was happily married also. It was over long ago, Kathryn. Don't let past things upset you. Doña Elvira is waiting with great joy to see her only granddaughter again.'

'I'm not really——' Kate began, and the smoothly beautiful face creased in smiles.

'You will be what she imagines you to be, my dear. We all tend to bend a little for her. I would guess that you do not relish a relationship with people you do not know too well, and I would also guess that Diego has already angered you. Try to forgive him. After Gerardo died, Diego was weighed down with the responsibility of this place, the many business interests of the family, and by and large with the added responsibility of two women and a younger brother. Overnight it seemed he was thrust into shouldering this heavy burden. He has carried it for years, and yet he is still only thirty-six. Javier is still more light-hearted. He has been able to be so because Diego allows it. I suppose he is giving him the freedom he did not quite have himself.'

'He's lord of all he surveys,' Kate said candidly, and Liliana nodded, no doubt hearing the hidden antagonism.

'That is true. But power carries with it responsibility, and Diego does not shirk that.' She suddenly laughed. 'I expect you are feeling some astonishment that I spend time trying to explain my eldest son? Someone must do it. He will never offer any explanations himself, and I already see danger signs between you. You resented him when you were little more than a child, but now you are probably more a match for him. Your time here must be tranquil, though—for Doña Elvira's sake. She adored Lucia. Like me, she did not have a daughter of her own, and a woman needs that, but she also adores Diego— probably too much—and she will be distressed should she realise that you dislike him.'

'I'm used to making my own decisions,' Kate said with a slightly embarrassed look at this outspoken woman. 'Your son, Señora Alvarez, is high-handed.'

'Call me Liliana.' She smiled at Kate with surprise and waved her hand. 'As to his being high-handed, Kathryn, it is his way. You will grow accustomed to it.'

Never in a million years, Kate thought, smiling a trifle wanly and following the servant from the room.

All she really wanted to do was get out of here, back to London and her work, and even the lovely room she was shown into did nothing to soften her outlook. The window looked out on to the courtyard at the front, and Kate stood watching the white doves as they wheeled and called around the splashing fountain. Even if this place *had* been the home of the Alvarez family for so many years, there was still the peace of the old monastery about it. All angry thoughts drifted away as she watched the late sunlight on the falling waters. Her mother must have missed this place.

Grief for her mother threatened to surface all over again, and tears came into her eyes almost without her knowledge. She sniffed impatiently. There had been enough tears already, and she couldn't afford to soften up. There was still Javier to face. If he still had the same inclinations she was going to rage, and once again she was sure she would be the one to take the blame.

There was a soft tap on the door and she looked around quickly, expecting one of the servants. 'Come in.' She hastily wiped the tears away from her cheeks, surprised that they had spilled over, and she was stunned to see the door open and find herself looking at Diego. Her fingers were a little more frantic then, as she tried to remove any sign of grief.

'Grandmother wishes to see you at once,' he said quietly. 'If you feel up to it, I will escort you to her suite.'

He waited for no reply, but stepped further into the room, and she nodded uneasily. He made her feel strange, he always had, and she was unsure why, except perhaps that he invariably angered her. She would have liked to ask him to go and come back later, and it did cross her mind to use the need to tidy herself up as an excuse, but he had walked up here to get her and she felt he would be none too pleased if she sent him on his way like a mere servant. There was time enough for trouble, and it would certainly happen.

'I—I'll come at once. If you could just give me a moment to——'

'I have intruded before you have even had the time to open your suitcase,' he murmured regretfully. '*Perdón*, Kathryn. It was thoughtless of me. I am sure that *Abuela* can wait for a little longer—at least until you feel refreshed.'

'No. No, it's quite all right. I'll come now.'

She stepped forward, her hands smoothing her bright hair with an uneasy little action that drew his glance to her face, and immediately he stopped. He had been turning to allow her to precede him through the door, and his abrupt stillness brought her closer than she would have liked. His gaze was on her face and the overbright look of her eyes. He had noticed her hastily stemmed tears, and she felt a flush of hot colour mounting in her cheeks as he simply stared at her.

Astonishingly, the hard, arrogant mouth softened. 'To travel so far is tiring. Tomorrow will be soon enough to see *Abuela*.'

'I prefer to see her now. I can rest later. She won't want to wait.'

'She is often impatient, but we are able to get around it quite easily.'

'There's no necessity. I'll come now.' She was a bit stiff, unable to soften at all to match his astonishing switch to gentleness, and he stiffened too, his eyes once more glittering and cool.

'Very well. I will take you to her.' He moved to allow her to precede him, and then once again stopped. 'Understand that any challenge to her, any harsh words——'

'I'm not a barbarian,' Kate said sharply. 'I'm not here to challenge anything. I just want to get this over and done with so that I can get back to London and my work.'

'You seem to have power. I know you are greatly prized by Merrol and Jones, particularly by Merrol.' His glance suddenly lanced over her. 'You do not exactly look like a female who wields power, but then perhaps my impression of you is coloured too much by the past. Appearances are deceptive, are they not?'

'They are indeed!' Kate stated firmly, marching out in front of him, extremely annoyed at the way his lips quirked with amusement. He was treating her like a simpering girl. He was going to get a shock.

'Are you not a little young to be in charge of so much important work?' he asked unexpectedly, closing her door as she waited for him in the passage. 'You restore castles in England, I understand?'

'Among other things, and I'm not young at all,' she snapped, her opinions of his attitude confirmed. 'I'm almost twenty-five!'

'I know. I have not forgotten.'

He was telling her with little subtlety that he remembered how she had made a fool of herself, and Kate blushed hotly. It had been easy to hurt her then. It wouldn't be now!

She followed him, her eyes on the broad shoulders and gleaming black hair. He walked like an athlete and there was that attitude of body that showed he was completely in control of everything. The vibrant sheen of sexuality probably never left him, but she hadn't been old enough to recognise it before. She would be glad to get a flight back to England. She was suddenly uneasy about being under the same roof as Diego Alvarez.

'*Abuela* does not now attempt the climb upstairs,' he said quietly as she walked uneasily by his side down the rather grand staircase. 'She has rooms on the ground floor. It is less trying for one of her age, and also it places her close enough to the chapel to make a journey there possible.'

'There's a chapel here?' Kate looked up in surprise and his glance skimmed her face.

'*Sí*. This was a *monasterio*. The chapel was restored many years ago. It is a comfort to *Abuela* to be able to go there. I am surprised you do not know. You seemed to be everywhere at once when you were seventeen. It amazes me that it escaped your attention.'

'I hadn't quite got around to prying that far,' Kate said sarcastically. 'You'll no doubt remember that we left rather precipitately.'

Damn! Damn! Damn! Why couldn't she hold her tongue?

'I had to see to it that you did. This quiet place needs no turmoil. If you had stayed, trouble would have ensued. It is my duty to see that *Abuela* lives out her life in tranquillity.'

His voice was quiet, but it seemed to slash out at her even so.

'My mother wasn't making any turmoil——' she began hotly.

'Did I mention your mother? Perhaps you have forgotten how Javier reacted to you? You were merely a young girl, a child almost. In any case, it would have been—unsuitable.'

A crushing remark—if she had now been crushable.

'I agree. He was at least twenty-three.'

'Twenty-one.' His lips quirked at her tone.

'Nearly as old as you,' Kate murmured scathingly.

'But not quite. I was twenty-eight and fast approaching the age of reason. Now I have reached it, and I look at you, Kathryn, and see fiery hair and a temper to match. I am no more indulgent than I ever was. Remember that *Abuela* is a very old lady. Allow her to see only the rose. I will take care of the thorns!'

He stopped at the door, the night-black eyes studying the pale, angry shape of her face, power etched strongly in his glance.

'You will show the delight to see her that she has to see you,' he ordered.

'I'll try, Señor Alvarez,' she said, bridling instantly.

'You will call me Diego. I am your cousin.'

'You are nothing of the sort and you know it!' Her voice was brittle with annoyance and he tilted her face, his strong fingers lightly touching her chin.

'I am whatever I wish to be,' he stated. His glance moved over the creamy beauty of her skin. 'You will discover that for yourself after a while.'

She had no time to point out that she would not be here long enough, because he threw open double doors and she was facing her grandmother—at least, she was facing the woman who wished to be her grandmother—and the man who called himself her cousin when he felt it convenient was holding her arm in a tight, warning grip.

CHAPTER THREE

KATE had already made her mind up about what she would see. It was a long time since she had seen Doña Elvira, and Diego had reminded her that she was now very old—too old to go upstairs. Kate had imagined a darkened room, perhaps too warm, the rather imperious old lady sitting in bed. She had expected to feel inside herself some instant antagonism, but she felt nothing like that and, as she relaxed, Diego's hold on her eased.

The room was at the back of the house, its two huge windows overlooking the valley, and now, in the evening, the room was brightly lit, the scent of flowers and perfume hanging in the air, and none of the expected heavy and depressing atmosphere of a sick-room for a very old lady.

The great windows were partly open to the night air of the valley, but Doña Elvira sat before a fire that crackled and flared merrily. She was dressed in black, her tiny frame almost lost in the huge chair. She seemed to have shrunk to doll-like proportions since Kate had last seen her, white hair piled on top of her head, the glitter of jewels at her throat, and small, bony hands folded in her lap on the blackness of the long skirt that almost hid her feet.

There was nothing wrong with the bright black eyes that fixed themselves on Kate, though, and Kate stiffened momentarily at the piercing look.

'Do not let your courage desert you at the last minute,' Diego murmured very quietly, his grip on her arm tight-

44

ening. 'She is not so fierce as she looks, and she expects no trouble. See that there is none.'

He led her forward; his face softened as he smiled at the old lady.

'*Abuelita*, I have brought Kathryn home.'

Doña Elvira looked a trifle frustrated.

'I cannot speak in English, Diego. You will have to translate.'

'Kathryn's Spanish is more fluent than ever, *Abuelita*,' he said, as if he was proud of the fact. 'She does not need anyone to speak for her.'

He meant, no doubt, that she was too outspoken, but Kate did not have time to give him a nasty look. Doña Elvira was delighted.

'So my *nieta* has come home,' she said softly.

Kate found herself walking forwards to look down at the woman who wished to be her grandmother, and for the moment all rebellious thoughts fled. There was no mistaking the joy on the haughty old face that turned to her, and a lump rose in her throat as she thought of the unhappiness that had come from her mother's misguided feelings of love for Diego's father. There was a moment of fear too. She had not come home. This was not her home in any way, and this old lady would have to be hurt all over again.

'I'm glad to see you, Doña Elvira,' she said in Spanish, her voice softening. 'Perhaps tomorrow we can speak together for much longer?'

'Yes, tomorrow. You speak beautiful Spanish, Kathryn. It will be easy to talk to you without the permanent presence of other people. I had thought that perhaps you would have forgotten your own language.' The small face tilted to Kate, the black eyes gleaming.

'Sit beside me. You are tall and it is a strain to look up at you. From here I cannot see anything of you.'

Instantly there was a footstool by Kate, and Diego drew back, watching intently as she sat and faced the dark, piercing eyes. She wanted to point out that Spanish was not her language, that this was not her home, but the black eyes that watched her contained too much joy for her to wipe any of it away. She felt terribly trapped.

'You were never like Lucia in your colouring. You seem to have not one shred of Spanish in you, even less as you have grown, but you have her shape of face, her sweet mouth. This strange colouring is from your father?'

'Yes, he was very fair.'

'And together they made a child with hair like fire. It is astonishing, is it not?' The piercing eyes roamed over her face and then fastened on her own blue eyes intently. 'She continued to be happy, Kathryn? She loved this man—this John Hart?'

'She loved him and she was very happy,' Kate said softly. Memory came racing back and tears rose in her throat. She blinked quickly, looking away.

'You are very beautiful,' Doña Elvira said softly. 'It is good to be with people who love you, is it not? You have felt love all your life, and now you are alone. My grandson tells me that you are very clever, with exceptional talent. When we talk tomorrow you must tell me about your work. I am too old to go to England and see it for myself, but I will hear it from your lips and imagine it.'

Sadness twisted Kate's heart again. Diego had sent them back to England, because of her. Perhaps if her mother had been able to come here regularly... Was she, like her mother, so filled with the passionate desire to get her own way that she could also be destructive?

The small, bony hand clasping hers surprised her.

'You are hurting, child. I know all about hurt. Perhaps also, as Diego said, you are very tired. I will see you tomorrow and we will talk.'

As Kate looked up there were tears in the bright old eyes, tears that matched her own. A small tear escaped and trickled down the wrinkled face and Kate's slender fingers covered the frail old hand.

'I'll see you whenever you feel up to it. Goodnight, *Abuela*,' she said softly. She stood and turned away as the old lady nodded, her dark eyes turning to gaze into the fire, and Diego signalled to a woman who had stood silently at the side of the room.

'I will leave *Abuela* in your care as usual, Ester,' he said softly. 'Do not leave her; she seems to be upset.'

He seemed to be blaming Kate for the old lady's tears, and right at this moment she had too many of her own to contemplate a battle with him. As he led her out of the room she walked quickly away along the passage.

'Kathryn!' He called to her, but she ignored him, reaching the stairs and running quickly up, hoping that she could find her own room without any help. Right now she wanted to be alone, and the dark, powerful Spaniard was the last person she needed near her.

She found her room at once and almost ran inside, closing the door and walking quickly over to the window, flinging it open to the night air. The last light was fading, the doves had settled to rest, and the only sound was the soothing fall of water from the fountain in the courtyard, but at this moment nothing would soothe her at all. She had been shocked to see tears on that frail old face. Doña Elvira was not as she had imagined at all. Eight years ago she had been too confused herself to even think about things deeply.

She wished she had not come. It brought her own grief back, and she felt guilt as if it was a legacy left to her, as if she owed it to everyone to correct a wrong brought on by her mother's mistaken passion. She covered her face with her hands and tears came again as she bowed her head. She felt impatient with herself. It was all because of tiredness; it had to be that. She should be angry instead of guilty. Nobody had come to the funeral, not one person who spoke her mother's language, only English friends.

A slight sound had her spinning round to see Diego standing in the open doorway, watching her sombrely.

'What do you want?' she asked sharply, her hand coming to wipe away tears yet again. 'I never heard you knock!'

He ignored her sharp words and simply looked at her steadily. '*Abuela* is right. You are hurting. It would have been better to leave you to rest before dinner. My grandmother could have contained her impatience. Also, I have not been particularly kind. Please forgive me. You are welcome here. I will see that you are made comfortable.'

Kate turned back to the courtyard, her shoulders stiff with the need to control her emotions. 'Thank you. I shall only be here for a short time.'

'Perhaps *Abuela* will wish you to stay forever. She imagines that this is your home,' he murmured softly. 'You have brought tears to her eyes and you weep yourself. Perhaps this was meant to be.'

'I've got a life of my own,' Kate reminded him, her heart beating quickly with an almost unbearable wave of fright. 'I have no intention of staying here. You insisted and I came. I rely on you to get me out of here with the least upset to your grandmother.'

'You are prepared to rely on me?' he asked quietly. 'This is quite a turn-about of events, is it not? In any case, surely you remember that only just now you acknowledged that she is your grandmother too?'

'It was in deference to her age. You know that.'

'Do I? Am I supposed to know you, Kathryn? All I know is that we are on the edge of battle all the time, and that it is likely to continue because I fear that you are preparing to desert *Abuela* just as your mother did so many years ago.'

'I will *not* carry my mother's guilt!' She looked at him stormily and he smiled slowly, all power and knowledge in the dark eyes.

'You already carry it, and your tears prove it.' One brown hand cupped her face, his thumb stroking absently at the tears on her cheeks. 'Do not fear. We will release you. There is, after all, a lover in England, and your all-important work. Also you are not a creature for captivity. You are much too wild.'

He turned to go, but she couldn't leave it at that.

'Don't *you* feel any guilt?' she asked abruptly. 'Nobody here has even mentioned that my mother is dead. All this pretence of love, and yet there wasn't a single person at the funeral from this so-called family. *Abuela* is too old to travel, but you're not!'

He turned slowly and came back to stand looking down at her.

'We knew too late that she was dying,' he said quietly.

'That letter... the date was a whole month before my mother died, and she said quite clearly that she was dying. It was no secret; she knew it. She told you.'

'You are determined to be hurt, are you not?' he said slowly. 'Very well, Kathryn. I gave you the letter to read. I did not give you the envelope.' He took an envelope from his pocket and handed it to her. 'I should have destroyed it, but perhaps it is better this way. You are anxious to blame us. Blame me if you must, but do not blame *Abuela*. I came as soon as the letter arrived. It did not arrive for two months. By then she was dead and it was too late. Had our name not been so well known, it would not have arrived at all.'

'Two months?' Kate looked at the letter. It was written to Señora Elvira Alvarez, but the address was not the *monasterio*. It had been to Albacete—miles and miles away. She looked up at Diego, and he was watching her carefully.

'She was born there and she knew it, but she had never been back,' he said softly. 'For some reason it was in her mind.'

Kate turned sharply away, but it was too late; Diego had seen the look on her face. He took her shoulders firmly and turned her back.

'Finally she did not remember, did she?' he asked quietly.

'No.' Kate looked down, avoiding his eyes. 'She had times when she remembered, but——'

'And she did not remember you either in the end.'

It was no question. He knew. Some helpful neighbour...

'No.'

Tears came flooding to the surface, the last of her grief, and she didn't even notice when he pulled her close, enfolding her in strong arms as she wept against his chest.

It was the first comfort she had had, the only comfort, and for a moment she forgot who this was as the tears and the strong arms drained the tension from her. His hand stroked her hair as she turned her face against his strength and warmth, the pain easing.

'*Pobrecita.*' His deep voice was soft, unchallenging, but she came to her senses, pulling away like a startled animal. What was she doing, letting this man hold her and murmur quietly? If she had an enemy, he was the one.

'I'm not a little anything,' she said stiffly, 'and I don't need comforting.'

'You have said so already, in England. Do not worry. You merely forgot for a moment.'

He was gently amused, and he took out a white hand-kerchief and wiped her tears away.

'And don't mop me up as if I were a child!' she snapped, backing off rapidly.

'I do not think of you as a child—not now.' He gave her an ironic look and turned away again. 'Now that the storm is passed, rest for a while and then dine with us. A shower, a change of dress and you will be able to last out long enough to have your meal with us. I realise that I have annoyed you, and it will convince me that you are not still wildly angry with me.'

'Then you're very easy to convince!' Kate said testily, glaring at him through her remaining tears.

'Perhaps I am,' he agreed softly. 'At this moment, though, there is more of the rose about you than the thorn, even though you gaze at me like a small fiery tiger. *Abuela* seemed to see it too. Perhaps you are tameable? In any case,' he added deliberately, 'there is Javier to face. It would be better to face him now and get it over with, every hurdle at once, eh?'

He simply walked out at that, and she was glad to see him go. He was pretty good at unnerving her—his final remarks had done that neatly. She didn't feel up to facing Javier. Since she had arrived she had steadily been softening up, guilt, grief and uneasiness all mixed up inside. Diego was to blame. She was not an inexperienced girl, but the night-black eyes were hypnotic. It would be too easy to become altogether fascinated by such a man.

Dinner was going to be an ordeal, but Kate wasn't about to back away from it. She took his advice and went to some considerable trouble to dress well. Cream suited her, and she had a very expensive dress that clung in all the right places and then flared around her. It was long enough to be suitable should they dress very formally for dinner.

They did. The first person she saw as a servant escorted her to the *sala* was Diego. He was, as usual, sardonically handsome, wickedly so in dark trousers and white dinner-jacket. He looked at her intently, his dark eyes inspecting her, but he made no move to rescue her as she stood uncertainly in the doorway.

Liliana did the rescuing. She moved forward graciously, her deep blue dress in soft folds around her.

'Come, my dear. What will you drink? I assume that Diego is poised to offer you anything you wish for?'

She gave a wry look in Diego's direction and relayed Kate's order when she asked for a sherry.

'Meanwhile, you remember Javier?' She turned Kate to where a handsome man, younger than Diego, stood watching, and his face creased in smiles as he came forward. He hadn't changed much. The handsome charm was still there, and she was aware of something she had never noticed when she was younger. He was spoilt.

'*This* is my cousin Kathryn?' he asked with good-humoured mockery. 'What have I done to deserve this delight? It must have been something very good to bring this sort of reward. You were always beautiful, but you are now alluring.'

'If Kathryn is to be shared, then Doña Elvira will take the lion's share,' Liliana said quickly. 'Do not start making demands on her time, Javier——'

'It would be unwise,' Diego cut in coolly, handing her a drink. 'She appears to be determined to leave. Naturally while she is here she will spend most of her time with *Abuela*. Things,' he added coldly, 'will remain tranquil.'

He looked at Kate with night-black, glittering eyes and it was like looking into the past. She almost shivered, and a soft flush of embarrassment coloured her cheeks. Javier seemed to find it all amusing, although he said nothing. He could afford to be amused. She was the one who had been blamed before for his misdeeds.

'Perhaps she can be persuaded to stay?' Javier said with a considering look at her. 'This is not London, but there is plenty of excitement in the area if you know where to look for it. I was not allowed to take her out too far before.'

Her cheeks flushed even more when she caught Diego's eyes on her, his gaze narrowed and challenging. He looked at her steadily and then turned his attention to his brother.

'Kathryn is no longer a child,' he said sardonically. 'She also has a very high-powered job in England and—commitments.'

For a moment she had thought he was about to begin relating his account of her 'lover', but he was merely skirting around it to get her on edge; his dark eyes acknowledged it. Fortunately dinner was announced, and Javier took her arm before anyone could make a move.

'Tell me about this job you have, Kathryn,' he murmured, leading her off with every intention of having her to himself. She was torn between wanting to escape from Diego's probing stare and wanting to establish that she was not now young and too afraid to stop Javier in his tracks. From his greeting and the way he was looking at her, no doubt that part would come before too long. For the moment she felt the need of a bulwark between herself and Diego Alvarez. She would have preferred it to be Liliana.

'We should ask Kathryn's advice about the *sala grande*, don't you think?' Liliana said later as they took coffee. 'It is the one thing that has not been touched— apart from the chapel, and that was done so long ago that it looks jaded.'

'You are hoping that she will consent to stay and work on it?' Diego asked ironically. 'I doubt if such a large English firm would be interested in our faraway *monasterio*.'

Little did he know, Kate thought thankfully. She could almost sense Felix at her shoulder whispering about his 'toe-hold' in Spain.

'Perhaps Kathryn would like to see it, all the same,' Liliana suggested. 'She will at least see what sort of renovation is required on old Spanish properties.'

'I would like to see it,' Kate said quickly, hoping that Liliana would escort her and get her away from both Diego and Javier. 'I wish you would call me Kate, too. Everyone else does.'

'I will take you to see the *sala*, Kate,' Javier said with a smile, but Diego's voice cut across her murmur of anxiety.

'I will take Kathryn,' he insisted quietly. 'You have some reports to finish before morning, I believe, Javier.'

'That's true,' Javier agreed, giving him an irritated look. He stood and took Kate's hand, raising it to his lips. 'As you can see, Kate, I am constantly overworked.'

She didn't think so. He looked altogether too relaxed. That spoilt look had come from somewhere, and Liliana had already said that Diego shouldered most of the responsibility himself to give Javier freedom. She could have thought that he was laying up trouble for the future, but she had no doubt at all that if trouble ensued Diego could cope more than adequately. It would be other people who would have to struggle with Javier—people like herself.

She wondered why Diego was insisting on showing her this *sala grande*. No doubt he was being very careful to shelter his brother from her disruptive character. Whatever it was, she knew it was not her he was thinking of protecting. He hadn't been thinking of her eight years ago, either.

At any rate, having shown enthusiasm to see the place, she was in no position to refuse to go, and she shot a glance at Diego that was irritated and cool. She noted well that he had deliberately chosen to stick to the more formal version of her name, and she remembered the reason he had given earlier. The thought tightened her lips and she turned to walk with him to the door, hoping to keep the viewing down to the minimum time possible.

It was a room that overlooked the courtyard. She assumed that from the direction they took, but as Diego opened the door and stood aside for her to enter all assumptions faded. He had flicked on a light, and she stepped into the most fantastic room she had ever seen.

It towered above her, obviously filling the whole height of the *monasterio* at this point. It was vast, a long, echoing room with a vaulted ceiling and arched windows that ran down one side. It was supported by slender pillars that disappeared into the dark arches of the roof, and Kate just stood there in the doorway, her blue eyes wide and fascinated.

'My goodness!'

She walked slowly forward, her footsteps echoing on the huge stone flags of the floor, her gaze anxious to be everywhere at once.

'What was this, the refectory?' she murmured to Diego without turning.

'Yes, it was. I see you know enough about buildings of this sort to recognise that.'

He wasn't exactly being sarcastic, but Kate had the desire to snap at him. She resisted it. Partly because the room fascinated her, and partly because she realised that she had to try to get on with him a little better. It was certain that *he* wouldn't be making any effort in that direction.

'I'm well trained,' she said quietly, ignoring his mockery. He was standing behind her, and a shiver threatened to run down her spine. He made her feel defensive and she concentrated hard on the room, her eyes moving upwards, peering into the gloom. 'Are there more lights?'

'Certainly.' He moved back to the door and flicked further switches, and Kate's gaze was riveted on the arched ceiling, seeing as she had half expected the faded, damaged finery of large, beautiful frescos.

'Original,' she whispered, almost reverent in her manner, her uneasiness forgotten. 'They're priceless.'

'You see why this room has been left,' he murmured, coming to stand beside her, his dark eyes on the faded glory of the roof. 'To undertake the necessary work on this room would be a challenge and a grave responsibility. A choice of the wrong people could wipe out centuries of beauty.'

'Yes.' Kate's voice was rather vague. She was too busy studying the room, and she walked away to inspect the walls, great high walls made from mellow stone, the same stone that looked so attractive from the outside. Here and there was plaster, peeling and dull, and, almost without realising it, she began to visualise this great room as it could be, her enthusiasm bubbling up, showing in her eyes and the entranced expression on her face.

'It is large, but not so large as Belton Castle,' Diego said quietly, and she spun round as the familiar name seeped through.

'How do you know——?' she began, and he looked down at her in sardonic amusement.

'I found you, if you recall, because people were willing to tell a confused foreigner where you worked. I hardly thought it suitable to burst in and demand a conference there. I did, however, have a talk with the receptionist at Merrol and Jones. She told me about your work and about Belton Castle. Having time to kill, I went to view it. They have opened it to the public—did you know?'

Kate ignored the mocking enquiry. She was too busy being angry that he had stalked her like a hunter, had charmed information from a receptionist who was normally extremely proper and strait-laced and had then had the gall to go along and check up on her ability.

'I see.' She took a deep breath, her decision to attempt to be friendly fading with every second. 'I hope you found the castle to your liking?'

'I did. I wished to see for myself if your talent was indeed exceptional. It is.'

'Thank you for your vote of confidence,' Kate snapped. 'Thank you too for showing me this room. If you don't mind, I'll go to bed. I'm very tired.'

'Certainly.' He gave an ironic bow. 'Emotion is tiring too, is it not? Especially when it is unwanted anxiety and barely controlled anger.'

'Why should you imagine that I'm angry?' Kate asked tightly, walking to the door. 'I enjoyed looking at the *sala grande*.'

'And planning it in your head,' he added quietly. 'I am very interested to realise that you think on the grand scale. It is surely unusual in a woman, this sweeping imagination coupled with the ability to carry out the dreams?'

'I've no idea if it's unusual,' Kate said irritably. 'I work with men.'

'It is understandable,' he murmured drily. 'You have the ability to disguise your femininity behind a very sharp tongue. No doubt they think of you as formidable.'

He made her feel like a female sergeant major, and she shot him a glance that would have withered a less arrogant male.

'I have enough feminine wiles to get my own way when orders fail,' she said irritably. 'Fortunately they're rarely needed. I'm an expert, with the backing of a large and prestigious firm.'

She didn't add that she got on very well with all kinds of people. He would never believe it, and she certainly wasn't proving it with him, and he was looking at her with that intent, powerful arrogance, amusement flickering in his eyes. 'Artists of all kinds are solitary people, I understand.'

'Your understanding clearly doesn't cover all artists,' Kate murmured, walking out into the dimly lit passage and anxiously trying to locate the stairs. 'The work I do can't be done in solitude. We need to employ a small army of workmen. I don't paint walls.'

'You do not like to dirty your hands?' Diego's eyes lingered on the slender length of her arms, making her uneasily aware that the dress she had chosen to wear showed satin-smooth shoulders.

'I'm paid to use my head.'

His eyes moved to the shine of her brilliant hair, lingered, and then moved over her face slowly, and he smiled with barely concealed satisfaction as more colour flooded into her cheeks.

'You are clever, little cousin. I acknowledge it. Does this—lover of yours realise your worth?'

'We're in the same line of business,' she told him, giving him a sparkling glance. 'We—appreciate each other.'

If he thought the worst she might as well confirm it.

The dark eyes flashed with something that was neither disdain nor anger. No doubt he did not appreciate it when she gave as good as she got. If he kept on attacking her she was finally going to have a go at him in no uncertain terms. She knew her own character well enough, and she had this burning desire to fly at him. He made her feel almost violent.

'Tomorrow you will see *Abuela*,' he said, changing the subject as she came at last to the divided flight of stairs. She wasn't sure if that was an order or a question, and she turned as she stood on the second step, looking down at him.

'Yes. Then I'll go home. Have no fear, I shall be very gentle with her.'

'Do not be fooled by her appearance. She has a will of iron. She likes her own way and has a very cunning ability to get it. Like you, she has her tactics when all else fails. I would say that you had inherited her character if I did not know better. I can only repeat my warning. She may not wish you to leave yet.'

'You brought me here,' Kate said heatedly, glaring down at him as he stood with upturned face watching her anger grow. '*You* will get me out of here!'

'She is my grandmother and I try to indulge her every whim. As you have already noticed,' he added sardonically, 'my brother would also be distressed.'

He appeared to be threatening in a very veiled manner, and she could see now that she should never have allowed herself to be talked into coming here. For one thing, she had known right from the first that Diego Alvarez was filled with derision towards her. For another, if Felix ever knew about that *sala grande*, she would be stranded here working, because he would push for business as hard as he could.

'I'm capable of getting myself back to the airport,' Kate said shortly, turning away. 'I'm very resourceful.'

'It is a long way,' he murmured mockingly.

'I'll use my feminine wiles,' she snapped.

He had got her back into this state of mind where her heart threatened to beat itself frantic, and she wanted to get to her room fast. She moved quickly, but got no further than another step before the dark voice stopped her.

'You are planning to go, but if *Abuela* wishes it I will bring you back.'

The quietly spoken threat had her spinning round to face him as he stood looking up at her. She was angry and alarmed, but she found it not quite so easy to look down at this particular man and keep him in his place. Height in this case was not a lot of use. His whole being dominated her. She was trembling and she resented it very much. She felt instinctively that she was being drawn into something that she would have to fight free of. He was dangerous and completely sure of his own power. He was even drawing her into the strength of it.

'I won't be either frightened or pressurised!' she seethed, her eyes wild, her hands clenched at her sides. 'When I wish to leave—I *will* leave!' He simply stared up at her, his dark eyes narrowed, his perfect mouth quirking with satisfied amusement.

'Be reasonable, little cousin,' he murmured sardonically. 'I searched for you and found you. I then waited a whole week before you came. It is not entirely justifiable to leave within one day, even for someone as headstrong and wilful as you.'

She leaned towards him angrily. She had taken as much as she was about to take, and he saw it in her eyes.

'I am taller, stronger and a man,' he warned softly, his eyes gleaming darkly. 'I also have a wicked temper, and would not hesitate to discipline my cousin should she behave like a wildcat.'

He looked as if he would enjoy handing out this hypothetical discipline. There was something indefinable gleaming in those eyes, but luckily Kate was saved as Javier came into the hall, moving with almost the same silent tread as his brother, but looking less like a dangerous jungle creature. He looked intrigued, suspicious and faintly annoyed.

'Have I interrupted a quarrel?' His eyes moved from one to the other, noticing their tense stance, no doubt too feeling the antagonism that hung like thunder in the air.

'You are interrupting nothing!' Diego said briefly, his eyes never leaving Kate.

'That is a relief. If you fight with her she will not stay, and I have not yet got to know her again. I intend to get to know her.' He smiled at Kate in a way that she had dreaded, and her heart sank one more notch. Oh, lord! She could do without this.

'Keep away from him,' Diego bit out quietly as Javier left. 'It would not be a good idea if he became attracted to you again. We have been through that once before!' He was no longer amused, and neither was Kate.

'No. *I've* been through it once before!' she snapped. 'I'm more capable of dealing with him now, though, and you can follow that advice and keep away from me also. We disliked each other on sight, and I must have been mad to agree to this trip.'

'Guilt brought you,' he reminded her smoothly. 'If I am to keep away from you, how am I to get you out of here? Only you and I know that you wish to flee from this place, desert your grandmother as Lucia deserted her, and hurry back to your work and your lover.'

'One ride to the airport is all I require from you,' Kate snapped. 'The rest I can handle myself—including my "lover"!'

'Of that last I have no doubt,' he said mockingly. 'I have already seen you handle him. He has my sympathy. You outclass him with ease. As to the rest, do not disappoint my grandmother because of your disapproval of me. I feel that at the end of her life she should be greatly indulged—even by a reluctant granddaughter.'

'I'm not any such thing, and——' Kate began, but he was as usual ready for any remarks.

'I am more than happy to agree with you on this point. I would not like you for a cousin. You are trouble, with your bright hair and your ready tongue. I had to act very speedily to prevent it before. This is a place of tranquillity.'

'Really. However do *you* manage to fit into it, then?'

'Perhaps I do not,' he murmured. 'Perhaps like you I am restless, frustrated and wishing to fight my way out of it. Unlike you, though, I recognise my duty.'

His dark eyes held hers with no effort at all, and she was stunned to feel an awareness race over her skin, the trembling return. She went up the stairs, fighting the desire to run and get out of his sight quickly.

'*Buenas noches*, Kathryn. *Hasta mañana.*'

His voice followed her softly, and she had to admit that the thought of him standing there, watching her with midnight-black eyes, frightened her in a very odd sort of way—a way that set her skin tingling.

CHAPTER FOUR

IT WAS like a run for cover. Kate almost raced into her room, closing the door and leaning on it for a second before resolutely getting ready for bed. Things were different now; *she* was different now. She would not let Diego intimidate her. Neither would she let herself be drawn into the wonder she had felt when she had known him before. All the same, as she lay in bed desperately wanting to sleep, she felt the quiet of the *monasterio* around her and unwanted memories came surging into her mind.

She had felt the quiet of the place then, when she was seventeen. Until she had come to this great house she had considered herself to be grown up, but Diego had put a stop to that. He had looked at her from his haughty height and had needed to say nothing at all to assure her that she was a child and a nuisance. She was romantically fascinated by him, but he rarely spoke to her.

At dinner, the only time he seemed to be there during the day, his dark eyes had looked at her coolly and intently, and she had felt completely out of place, her blushes seeming to fill him with quiet amazement.

He was out every day seeing to the business of the family, the property, the orchards inland, the vineyards in the Rioja, and she would have loved to go with him, to see some of the district around and to see more of her imperious, handsome adopted cousin. He never offered to take her, though. When he spoke to her he was carefully polite, calling her Kathryn, a name she hardly used, his eyes too dark and intense until she was almost ready to hide and give up the sight of him.

It was Javier who really paid attention to her while her mother spent time with *Abuela*. At first he only took her on short trips, his face amused as she tried to see everything at once, but gradually he took her further, facing his brother's disapproval with a wide grin when they came in too late for dinner several times.

Diego overwhelmed her, he was even a little frightening, but Javier was charming. He made her feel important, and she got used to his hand on her shoulder as he showed her things. She was only slightly alarmed when he put his arm around her one day. After all, he was almost her cousin.

Diego was not amused. For the first time he took her aside, cornering her as she walked in the gardens.

'It would be as well if you remembered that you are a child only, *señorita*,' he said sternly, hurting her when he dropped the use of her name and became even more formal. 'I do not know how you behave in England, but here you will behave decorously.'

She wasn't sure what decorously meant in this context, but she knew she was seventeen and hadn't done a thing wrong.

'I'm not a child, Don Diego,' she said firmly. 'I'll be eighteen next year.' It took a bit of courage to face him, but she did, her bright head held high.

'And still a child,' he said cuttingly. He frowned down at her. 'And do not use that ridiculous title. You are not a servant.'

Actually she had said it to placate him, and also because he seemed to be too important to address by his first name alone.

'Do you want me to call you *señor*?'

'Not unless you wish to anger me.'

'It wouldn't make any difference. You're angry with me already. You're always angry with me and I haven't done anything at all.'

She blushed and looked away when he stared at her in astonishment, and his cool fingers curved around her face, turning her to him.

'You can read my mind, *niña*? You wish me to fuss over you? I am very busy and, in any case, you will not be here for much longer.'

It sounded a bit like a threat, and she looked up at him, not having the nerve to snatch her face away from his imperious grip.

'Can't we come back again? Don't you like me at all?'

'I am not accustomed to seeing a bright-haired girl every time I turn my head,' he murmured, staring down at her with narrowed, dark eyes. 'You have the ability, *niña* to be in all places at once.'

It was no answer at all and she felt a wave of disappointment.

'I'm not. You hardly ever see me. I go out with Javier almost every day.'

His grip tightened and his eyes became cold again. 'That is why I remind you that you are a child still. My brother does not seem to be as much aware of that fact as I am. It would be as well if you were to stay in the *monasterio* and allow him to get on with his work.'

'I don't stop him. I just look around. I could go with you if you'd rather,' she added guilelessly, looking at him with serious blue eyes, hoping he would agree. He stared at her harder than ever for a second, and then his face softened.

'I would prefer that you were safely back in England,' he said gently. 'However, we will see. In two days I am going to the Rioja. It is a long way and I will not be back in the evenings. When I come back I will take you to the city. It is time you had a new dress for dinner.'

She blushed and her eyes sparkled happily, bringing a devastating smile to the lean, dark face.

'That makes you happy? You are greedy, *niña*?' His hand tilted her chin and she had to close her eyes to escape the dark gaze.

'No. I'm just happy about going with you.'

'Do not be too happy. I am too busy to become your full-time escort. We will see how the expedition goes. In the meantime, beware.'

She wasn't sure what she was to beware of, but she felt gloriously happy, and Diego actually spoke to her for a long time at dinner, to Javier's obvious astonishment and annoyance.

And it was Javier who spoiled it all, although she took the blame. While Diego was away, Javier changed. It was as if an unseen leash had been removed, and she suddenly didn't feel too safe with him any more. He kept her out late every evening, although she would have preferred to be back for dinner, and they were out when Diego came home.

She had been miserably uneasy all day, embarrassed at the way Javier treated her, but her embarrassment knew no bounds as they stopped in the courtyard and Javier pulled her into his arms. She was too stunned to resist, struggling very belatedly as his lips closed over hers. She hated it, but her ordeal didn't last long; another took its place.

The car door was jerked open and she found herself standing in the warm night air, Diego's hands tightly on her shoulders as he stood behind her and pulled her against him, raging at Javier who had sprung angrily from the car. Diego was so furious, his words so fast that she barely understood, but Javier stormed off into the *monasterio* and Diego spun her to face him, his hands not at all gentle.

He stared down at her, his face wild with rage and then he turned her to the door. 'Go to your room.' His voice was harsh, thick with anger.

'But I didn't——'

'Go!'

He turned away and she fled, running up the stairs to her room and closing the door, desperately hoping her mother would not come to say goodnight and be upset by all this. She was shaking from the ordeal and from the sound of Diego's anger. The last time she had seen him he had been gentle; now he was furious.

It was Diego who came, and it wasn't to say goodnight. He entered after a brief tap on her door and she turned to him with a very white face.

'I warned you about your behaviour,' he said sternly. 'Perhaps you now understand why. You will return to England.'

'You're sending us away?' she asked forlornly. 'I didn't do anything.'

'I am sending *you* away. Unfortunately, your mother will be included. If you were so anxious to remain here you should have taken my advice and behaved differently. As it is, the situation is now a little too far advanced. I can set down firm rules or I can get rid of you at once. I prefer the latter course. In England you may behave as you wish.'

'I behave just like any other person. I've never done anything wrong here. *I* didn't kiss Javier, it was the other way around, but I can see that I'm taking the blame.

You didn't come to see if I was all right, only to shout at me.'

'I am not shouting,' he pointed out coolly. 'I am sending you away because it is necessary.'

She didn't defend herself any more. It would have been pointless. He made her feel childish and edging on wickedness, and the stern, autocratic face was unbending, the night-black eyes cold.

'I'll be very glad to go,' she said quietly. 'If my mother comes again, I'll stay with my father. She probably won't come anyway. It's all too clear that we're not welcome.'

He hadn't corrected her. The next day they had left, and her mother had never come back. No doubt she'd thought she was being dispatched coolly, and Kate had never enlightened her—another source of guilt that lay at the back of her mind always.

Kate awoke next day feeling definitely jaded after a restless night when she had slept only fitfully. It was a problem that had been with her for months. She had watched her mother's swift decline into ill health after her father had died, and she had been powerless to stop the relentless slide from life that had finally left her alone. Trying to work and look after her mother had been an added strain, and finally she had moved out of her flat and back to her old home to spend all her time with her mother. There had been little chance of sleep.

It had all combined to leave Kate with breathless spasms of nervous tension. She knew it would go, once her life had settled back into some ordered routine, but it had been this that had lengthened her compassionate leave and she had told nobody at all.

It was amazing that she had not been breathless yesterday. Tense was a very inadequate word to describe her feelings when Diego was there, probing her mind, domineering and arrogant. If she had held her tongue instead of fighting back, she would have been more tense still.

Nevertheless, memories and annoyance had given her a bad night, and she was very relieved to find that breakfast was served to her in her room. When she enquired why, she was told that it was quite normal. Liliana Alvarez apparently always had breakfast in her own room, and this morning Javier and Diego were ready to leave early—the servant murmured that they had probably already gone.

It meant that if she should want to leave there would be no one to take her to the airport, and naturally she assumed that Diego had thought of this. On the other hand, it gave her a time without those dark and glittering eyes on her.

The day was beautiful, and she dressed in white ankle-length trousers and a dark green shirt and went straight down after breakfast to explore the outside of the *monasterio*. She resisted the inclination to view the *sala grande* in daylight. The fact that she was dying to get her hands on the project was something she would keep firmly under control. As far as she was concerned, the place didn't exist. Her life was in London, her job there, and she wanted no long sojourn in Spain under the saturnine gaze of Diego Alvarez.

The fountain sparkled in the morning sunlight and the doves were back again, their soft calling adding to the soothing music of the falling water. It all brought a smile to her face, and she walked beneath the towering walls to the back of the *monasterio* where the low wall guarded the long drop to the valley.

Her tight, breathless feeling was still there, but as she stood and gazed across the scene some of the tension eased. From this vantage-point the whole valley lay below her, and her hands came to the wall as she moved to look down.

Everything was reduced to miniature. The patches of brilliant greenery that were trees were so far below that they could not be clearly identified. A white church stood by a small village in the distance, and the whole red and gold valley could be seen from this towering crag. It was completely disorientating, an eagle-eye view, the feeling that for a second she was more than mortal, and in the distance the blue and green glitter of the sea, picking up the morning sunlight, finished off a breathtaking canvas of nature's artistry. Nothing had changed.

Her senses were suddenly inexplicably alert, a peculiar feeling racing through her, and Diego's dark voice brought a shudder to her skin, a reaction that had begun even before she had known he was there.

'At this moment, with the sunlight on you, you seem to have a halo of fire. It is fortunate that I am not superstitious or I would begin to imagine you had appeared from the clouds to inspect the *monasterio*.'

She couldn't even turn. His unexpected appearance when she had fondly imagined him miles away from the *monasterio* had caught her completely off guard. Hearing him so unexpectedly set her heart pounding, and the breathless tension raced back, draining any remaining colour from her face.

'What is wrong?' He sensed her distress, and she felt his hand on her shoulder. 'I have startled you?'

He turned her towards him and stared at her intently for a second, until she felt even worse, and something flickered in the black gaze as he let her go. She turned

away to look out across the valley, struggling to show
no sign of her difficult breathing.

'You are ill!' He wasn't asking her a question, and he
stepped close behind her, his hands coming to her
shoulders, the touch of his fingers warm through her
shirt.

Something indefinable seeped into her. It was unbe-
lievable. His hands moved surely but gently, and every
bit of tension drained away as if it had never been there.
Her breathing returned to normal, her long sigh a deep,
grateful breath.

'You have not answered,' he murmured. He turned
her back, and this time she was able to face him.

'I didn't know it was a question,' she managed mockingly. 'I assumed that, as usual, you had come to a
decision.'

Anger flared instantly behind his eyes and she rapidly
back-pedalled.

'I thought you'd gone ages ago.'

He relaxed visibly, the dark gaze sweeping over her
with lingering suspicion. He wasn't quite satisfied, she
could tell, but clearly he didn't want a battle this
morning, and neither did she.

She didn't like his hands on her. She hadn't liked it
yesterday, even when he had just been holding her arm.
She was no longer seventeen and fascinated by him, but
it gave her a feeling she had never felt before, as if sparks
and signals were passing between them, and she was glad
when he let her go, his probing gaze easing.

'It—it's very dry.' She was desperately trying to fill a
yawning gap in normal conversation, and he knew it.
He laughed softly.

'Rain will come and the land will spring to life. It is
not a desert. Things grow well even in the dry times.'

'What are those acres of stunted trees?' She pointed down into the valley and up the surrounding hills. 'They all look dead. I don't remember seeing them before.'

'They were there. They are almonds and not dead. Stay and I will prove it.'

'You know I can't stay.' Kate turned abruptly and walked towards the courtyard. 'I'll decide when I've seen your grandmother, but whatever I decide it will only be for a short time—another day at the very most.' She spun round to face him. 'It's very difficult. How can I see Doña Elvira when everyone seems to need your permission for even minor things? You're going out, and that leaves me hanging around just waiting for you.'

'I would hate to have you waiting for me impatiently,' he mocked. 'I have no doubt that *Abuela* will send for you. She has never yet felt that my permission is necessary when she wants something. I do not control her. In any case, I shall not be out for too long.'

He sounded mockingly indulgent, as if she were begging for an outing again. She wasn't approaching eighteen now, and she seethed at this patronising manner.

'Look, I'm not asking your permission either,' she said hotly. 'This is quite astonishing. I'm here to see your grandmother and nothing else. I've seen her. I'll see her again, and then I'll have to go. I can't have endless leave.'

'Would your attitude be the same if you had not clashed with me long ago? Would you have been content to stay a few days and admire the beauty you obviously enjoy if I were not here?'

'I'm a very busy person,' Kate said incisively, her face showing embarrassment.

'Too busy to spare time for your grandmother,' he noted coolly. 'I understand the pull of England in your

particular case, but do not imagine that I will allow you
to forget that you also have a duty here.'

'I don't have anything of the sort!'

'You have a duty to atone for Lucia's desertion. I
suspect that you are as disruptive as your mother was,
but for *Abuela's* sake I will not allow you to walk away
from that duty.'

'You're mad if you think you can order me about!'
In spite of her angry words, Kate felt again the shudder
of fear and a return to that breathless panic she had
fought all night and this morning. He was capable of
anything, and getting out of here was very necessary.

'I am merely reminding you that you also have a com-
mitment here,' he said coldly. His slight warmth had
totally gone. 'There is nothing to fear. You are under
my protection, as are all my family. I protected you once
before. You are my cousin and I acknowledge this.'

'You're too kind!' Kate said sarcastically. 'Your protection before was to send me packing. I'll settle for that
again.'

The cool lips smiled with arrogant mockery. 'This time
it does not suit my plans. *Hasta luego*, Kathryn. See to
it that you do not annoy me too much. England is far
away, may it remain so.'

To her astonishment, he took her hand and raised it
to his lips, but his smile was so sardonic that she would
have snatched it away had he not let it go first.

'I feel under no obligation to remain here,' she said
angrily, but he sauntered off to the front of the house
where the Lamborghini was now parked. His only reply
was a casual lifting of the elegant hand, and then he was
gone, a cloud of red dust marking his passage, and her
tingling fingers reminding her that he had indeed been

there. Her tension had once again eased, and astonishingly she knew it was because he had touched her hand.

It was almost frightening that he could make her feel like that. His going had left her almost with a pain. He had left smoothly and arrogantly, his leaving condescending in spite of his softly spoken words, and she had wanted to call him back. She hadn't finished with him yet. There was a lot more to say to him, but he made the decisions and he had managed to fill her with vague fears. He couldn't possibly have also made her feel restlessly excited, could he?

She walked back into the house and was just in time to see Doña Elvira being wheeled along the passage by the rather stern-faced woman who seemed to be her personal servant.

'Kathryn! You are already about. I thought I would have to wait impatiently for a sight of you. I do not now require much sleep, and I have been awake for some hours. I am afraid that I have finally lost patience and ordered Ester to bring me out of my room to search for you.'

The piercing old eyes were alight with amusement at this minor mischief, and Kate could do nothing but smile too. There was something about this woman that spoke of her mother, and she was reminded that the act of giving birth did not make a mother, it was caring, and this woman had cared enough to adopt Lucia when she was a baby. Why should she not remind her of her mother? What was wrong in feeling, as she was beginning to do, that this was her own grandmother?

She crushed the thought, horrified at the implications. To own Doña Elvira as her grandmother would be to commit herself to frequent and long visits to Spain and the *monasterio*—all very well, except that Diego was here, not to mention Javier.

'Something is wrong, Kathryn?'

The old lady looked at her a little anxiously, and Kate pulled herself together, realising that she had simply been staring and thinking. No doubt some of the horror of her conclusions had shown on her face.

'No, nothing.' She resisted the temptation to say *'Abuela'* although the name sprang very readily to her mind. 'I had rather a restless night. I'm a little dreamy.'

'Come back to my suite, then. We will have a steaming cup of chocolate. I am supposed to give it up, but it is the habit of a lifetime. What do they expect?'

The light shrug reminded Kate of Diego. He was beginning to insinuate himself into all her thoughts. She was only too happy to walk behind the chair as Ester turned it with no word and retraced her steps.

Kate thought later that the time with Doña Elvira was one of the happiest times she had spent for ages. The old lady was surprisingly lively, intelligent and bright, with an amusing cunning that showed how she managed to still get all her own way. Before the drinks were finished Kate found herself telling her all about her work in England, describing the stately homes, and even drawing sketches of them and the work she had done.

Doña Elvira was enthralled, her questions sharp and interested.

'Pass those photographs, Kathryn,' she said when Kate at last ran out of steam. 'I will show you your mother when she was small, and when she was a teenager.'

It was somehow comforting to look at the heavily framed old photographs, and they showed something of her mother that Kate had never noticed. The flashing eyes, the arrogantly tilted head, the face of a rich and secure Spaniard. She had changed after her marriage; the face had become more gentle, loving.

'She didn't look like this in England,' Kate said softly, her eyes never leaving the image of her mother.

'She was very wilful always when she was at home,' the old lady said with an unexpected chuckle. 'She was never easy to manage, but she was a delight to me. My husband died when Lucia was twelve, and then there were just the three of us. Gerardo, Lucia and I. We spoilt her. It was not wise, as it turned out.'

She pushed forward another photograph, and Kate found herself looking at Diego's father. He was not such a dominant figure as Diego. The same handsome face looked back at her, but he seemed to have a softer air.

'Lucia adored him,' Doña Elvira said quietly. 'She expected to marry him, and when Liliana appeared in his life Lucia fought like a wildcat. There were many scenes when she realised Gerardo's intentions. Liliana is gentle, and finally she ceased to come here and refused to see Gerardo. It was the breaking-point. I had to go myself to see Liliana and explain to her family. While I was away there was a dreadful confrontation between Lucia and my son. He stormed out, and when we both returned Lucia had gone. We traced her to the airport and to England, and we could never find another trace of her. She had lost herself in your great capital city. I heard nothing more of her until she came here. Later she wrote to me. It was then too late.'

Kate wanted to ask her why she had allowed Diego to send them away. Nobody mentioned it at all, and she couldn't bring herself to ask now. The old hands smoothed the frame and stroked over the photographs, and Kate felt again the weight of guilt that had been left to her.

'Don't distress yourself,' she said softly. 'She was happy, very happy. She met my father in London, and they were married as soon as he finished at medical school. I suppose she told you that when we were here. I know it doesn't give back all those years when you were worried, but now you know what happened.'

'At least there is you, Kathryn.' The old face smiled, and Kate just did not have the heart to deny it.

'Of course, *Abuela*,' she agreed. 'I work in London, but it's not too far away when I can fly out. I must go back soon, but I'll visit you often.'

'I'll be content with that,' Doña Elvira said quietly. 'I know you have a settled life of your own, but if I can think that the *monasterio* is your home, your real home, and that you will come often, then I am content.'

It seemed to cheer her up and bring her back to her earlier frame of mind, and when she suggested that Kate look at the chapel with her Kate was only too happy to agree.

Long before the sky darkened Diego returned, but made no appearance. Kate saw José and he informed her that Diego was with his grandmother. It gave her a peculiar pang of misgivings. Now he would know that she had consented to come here often. She had felt so close to Doña Elvira that for the moment she had forgotten the power of her so-called cousin, and now she was suffering great qualms. She dreaded seeing his sardonic satisfaction when he realised he had won. One thing at least—it gave her the chance to leave almost at once. Doña Elvira would now understand.

She was thankful when she entered the brilliantly lit dining-room that evening, after she had been called by a servant, to find that Diego had not arrived. Javier was there, though, and sprang up at once, that look on his face again. He was going to be trouble. She saw that clearly.

'All day, Kate!' he said with exasperated and bold humour. 'All day away from the house, and all the time you were here, no doubt quite lonely. I could have taken you to the city and we could have walked around like two tourists. Instead, I was dispatched to count oranges.'

'Hardly that,' Diego said sardonically, entering the room at that moment. 'That you were so late back makes me wonder if indeed you sat counting them.'

'The Dolce family are very hospitable,' Javier remarked.

'And they have two bright-eyed daughters,' Diego countered.

Liliana sat beside Kate and smiled at her sons. 'Don't worry about Kathryn. She had a long talk with her grandmother this morning, and since then she has been with me. We have walked in the gardens and had lunch together. It has been most pleasant.'

She smiled at Kate and patted her hand, but Kate was very busy being wary. Diego looked sardonically pleased with himself. She wondered what *he* had been doing.

As he sat elegantly at the head of the table later, the brilliantly dark eyes were turned on Kate.

'I am pleased that you have not been too bored, Kathryn.' She flushed with annoyance at his tone, so condescending. 'Your long talk today has left *Abuela* very happy. I have been to see her, and she is looking forward to tomorrow. She had to be persuaded to stay in her suite. She was excited enough to consider dining with us.'

'I—I expect it's due to the fact that she rarely has visitors,' Kate said hurriedly, wondering why he wasn't coming out with the fact that she had promised to keep on returning to Spain.

'Few that she approves of,' he agreed quietly.

After dinner Kate had to get it all out in the open. That tight, breathless feeling was coming back. Diego could ease it magically away, but she wondered if he wasn't the one who was causing it now.

'Can I speak to you for a minute?' she said quietly, as Liliana and Javier stood talking in the *sala* and prepared to take coffee.

'Certainly. I wish to speak to you also. Come to my study.'

Now what have I done? The words came to her mind and infuriated her. Was she admitting that she was scared of this man still? Certainly some odd feeling was coursing through her, and it was indicative of his power here that neither Liliana nor Javier questioned their sudden departure, although Javier looked distinctly irritated.

She walked beside Diego along a passage that ran opposite to the one she had traversed this morning, and she had not really got herself under tight control as he ushered her into a well-lit room. She had never seen it before. She had never even thought of coming in here when she was a 'child'.

The high walls were lined with books, most of them old. Any collector would have been overjoyed to walk in here, she was sure. The deep armchairs were dark red leather, and the desk that dominated the room was very old polished rosewood.

'I see that you are viewing it with the practical eye of the expert.'

Diego's deep voice jerked her back to the moment and the reason for being here.

'It's what I do. I'm afraid it stays with me. Perhaps one day it will quite ruin everything I see.'

'With you, I think not!' he said decisively, looking down at her. 'You are not quite as drily practical as that. And now, you wished to speak to me?'

'Yes. I've spoken to Doña Elvira, as you know. She understands that I have a life in England and that my work is there. I've promised to return to Spain regularly. I imagine that will satisfy your desire to see that I behave dutifully. Tomorrow I shall go back to London. I would be most grateful if you could arrange my trip to the airport.'

Kate was quite pleased with her little speech. It sounded most reasonable. He didn't think so, and his own speech was very brief.

'Regrettably, I cannot. You are to stay!'

CHAPTER FIVE

DIEGO wasn't smiling—not that there was anything to smile about—but there was a look of arrogant satisfaction about him that brought renewed fury to Kate's face. The need to throw herself at him came surging back through her body like a hot tide. Pure rage and frustration made her face pale, and his hand came to tilt her chin as the night-black eyes bored into her own.

'Think well before you attack me,' he warned softly. 'Subduing you would be little trouble. I told you last night that I would not hesitate to punish you, and your intentions are there in your eyes.'

'Tomorrow I shall go home!' she managed in a choking voice, fighting to contain her rage, the breathlessness growing almost out of control.

'You are to stay. You seemed to me to be very interested in the great *sala*. The task of refurbishing it is yours. This morning I rang Merrol and Jones. They were delighted to have the contract to do the work, delighted also that you were on the spot. Señor Merrol will arrive tomorrow to discuss the whole thing with us. I will stay at home and be there to add my own thoughts on the subject.'

'Felix? Felix is coming here?'

Nothing else seemed to sink in, and his dark eyes noted it coldly.

'Surely you are not surprised? I was not at all astonished that he leapt at the chance to be here with you, even if only for a day.'

'Then you'll no doubt realise, while you're busy playing Cupid,' Kate said acidly, 'that he will do anything for me, anything I ask, including taking me home at once!'

'That will be unlikely,' he said coldly, all the amused derision dying from his handsome face. 'Knowing your hold over this man, I have made it quite plain that the only way the work will be given to them is if you do it yourself. He was most agreeable to that. Apparently they have been wanting to get a foothold in this country for some time. I promised to assist them. He seems to me to be a very hard-headed businessman, and I think that even as your lover he will not allow you to refuse the work.'

That just about did it! He thought he could order her about like a peasant, and she was sick and tired of having Felix pushed down her throat. He wanted her here for *Abuela's* sake, and he was determined to keep her, just as he had been determined to get rid of her before. He did exactly as he liked all the time, and it was so unfair that rage choked her. She flew at him, giving way to the urge that had surfaced more than once.

Rage didn't help at all with Diego. He caught her up, lifting her completely off her feet, one hand coming to cup her face in a grip that could be called nothing less than cruel.

'So at last I really see Lucia's daughter. An inherited rage that surfaces when things are not to your liking. I cannot say that I am surprised. Since we met again you have had this desire to fly at me. You have been smouldering inside. You wish to wear yourself out? You may begin!'

With one of his arms tightly restraining her, and the hand like steel holding her face still, there was not much that Kate could do in the way of wearing herself out. She had to admit, too, that she was scared. Aggressive masculinity had always been recognisable just beneath the surface with Diego, but now it was being allowed to rampage freely, his dark eyes flaring into hers.

'Let me go! How dare you?'

She had meant to sound outraged, but she was quite capable of hearing her own voice, and it simply sounded weak and shaken.

'The daring was yours, I think. Either you are presuming upon our faint relationship to display such boldness, or you are given to behaving in any way you choose. Whatever your reasons, it is a mistake to presume too far with me.'

His hand slid from her aching face into the fiery shine of her hair, twisting hard as he brought her head to his. The sharp tug brought tears to her eyes, but he didn't even notice. The hard, sensuous mouth clamped down on hers, cutting off her gasp of anger as his other arm fastened her to him tightly.

There seemed to be a fiery recognition in both of them, almost a desire to punish each other bitterly. It was an antagonism that had been there as they had met again in England, and it had not lessened. She resented the way this man could wield power over her, and she hated this harsh, masculine way of forcing submission. She had never been kissed in this hateful way before, nor ever felt her strength drain away as it was doing now.

Even so, a strange relaxed feeling began to seep into her, her legs shaking, and Kate murmured anxiously against the hard lips as they began to probe more deeply. The sound brought instant release, but not from the tight arm that held her.

For a second she could only stare into the eyes that were so close to her, and then her hands pushed against his chest—with less strength that she would have liked.

'Let me go,' she gasped shakily. 'You have no right to——'

'Rights sometimes become lost in the surge of the moment,' he murmured, his eyes still holding hers. His glance slid to her lips that were bruised and trembling. 'Perhaps Lucia needed such treatment, but who was here to hand it out?'

'She was gentle,' Kate began, but he looked sceptical and stepped away from her.

'Perhaps she was—after her husband had subdued her. Rage is still clearly in her genes.'

'And in yours!' Kate snapped, beginning to feel outrage again as the odd relaxed feeling drifted away and anger replaced it.

He glanced at her sardonically, a faint glint of laughter at the back of the glittering look. 'You attacked me, if you recall. As I have never been disposed to take a beating, I had two choices—to either kiss or slap you into a different frame of mind. Perhaps next time you would state your choice?'

'There'll be no next time!' Kate stated, turning her flushed face away from the ironic gaze. 'I'm going home, and there's nothing you can do about it.'

'*Abuela* is joyous that you are here, and it is your duty to stay. That you feel the need to earn your own living is unfortunate, but for the time being you can earn it here.'

'What do you mean—that I feel the need to earn my own living?' Kate snapped, swinging round to face him. 'Just what exactly are you proposing—that I give up my career and comfort *Abuela*?'

'It would be as honourable,' he bit out. 'You have just proved yourself to be Lucia's daughter in no uncertain way. That kind of fire brought havoc here and heartbreak, but I am here now, not my father, and I would have no difficulty in controlling you. Your presence would be a joy to *Abuela* that would last for the rest of her life. She has earned joy and you can give it.'

'Until two weeks ago, *Abuela* and this place were merely a vague memory at the back of my mind,' Kate said frustratedly. 'I have a settled life, one that I enjoy. I live in an exciting city and do an exciting job. I won't even think about staying here.' She turned away again, willing to admit that she was still very shaken from such close contact with him. 'I'm disappointed in *Abuela*,' she added softly. 'She was wonderful to me today.'

'She knows nothing of this. I control the *monasterio*, and have done so for years. Everything is my responsibility, including the happiness of those who live here. I have decided to have the *sala grande* refurbished, and I have chosen the firm. She will be delighted that it is you who are to do it. To use an English expression, it kills two birds with one stone.'

'You were glad to get rid of me once.'

'As a child, you were a responsibility I did not need. You are a woman now, responsible for yourself.'

'And what about my happiness? You haven't given any thought to my wishes or my comfort,' Kate pointed out bitterly.

'I will see to it that you are comfortable. There is a great deal of luxury in this place, or hadn't you noticed?' His face hardened, the amused look dying. 'As to happiness, it is easily gained by thinking of others and fulfilling your duties. *Abuela* has less time left to her for happiness than any of us.'

For a second they stared at each other like enemies circling for an advantage, and Kate's lips tightened.

'I'll stay. I'll do the *sala grande*, more because you think I can't than for anything else, but you can look out for trouble if anything at all annoys me. You can forget that recent line of subduing me, or you'll find that you've bitten off more than you can chew.'

'You imagine so?' The perfect lips quirked with amusement. 'I can handle you, firebird.'

'I'll not even speak to you unless it's really necessary!' Kate snapped, her face flushed.

'Or until you again feel the need to fling yourself at me with claws extended,' he added with an infuriating low laugh. 'As you have agreed, I will go and let *Abuela* know. She will sleep more happily. Do you wish to come with me?'

'I do not!' Kate stormed out, regardless of whether or not he had finished talking to her. She was too upset to face the others. In her room she felt safe, until she remembered those arms and the way his touch could drain both tension and anger from her. She would have to avoid Javier too. He was looking all too interested. How she could be expected to work in this atmosphere was beyond her, but she would do it. She would show Diego Alvarez that she was a match for him any day. As to Javier, she could deal with him. She had dealt with plenty of wolves; a Spanish wolf was no worse than any other.

Kate came down to breakfast next day to find that Diego had already neatly spread the word, leaving her no chance to back out of it. Today apparently everyone was at home, and breakfast was served in the small and cosy dining-room that led from the more grand one used at night.

'So you are staying, Kate? I will get to know you again. We will go out together.'

Javier was looking smugly pleased with himself, and Kate had the desire to put him in his place right then, until she saw Diego's face. His suddenly thunderous looks gave her the chance to annoy him and get back at him for a very uneasy night.

'I really would love to get around and see some of Spain,' she murmured eagerly. 'When I'm not too busy, I'll go with you.'

Javier moved his chair closer and Kate's eyes slid to Diego, her mouth quirking with the need to contain laughter as his face darkened even further with annoyance.

'But not today,' he said coldly. 'Today we wait for Kathryn's—friend.'

For once it didn't annoy her. If he thought she was prepared to encourage Javier and also keep Felix dangling, then let him! She would not upset either *Abuela* or Liliana. Nothing prevented her from upsetting Diego, though, and nothing would give her greater satisfaction. If he thought he could storm into her life, order her out here and keep her here, he would find he had stirred up more trouble than he could handle. This time, though, there would be no outbursts like her mother's. This time she would let him find out the hard way, a little at a time. She seemed to have plenty of time, because she knew that Felix would never agree to giving this contract up.

'I should perhaps go and see Doña Elvira before the day becomes too hectic,' Kate murmured, and Diego nodded his stern approval, getting up too as she rose from the table.

'Do not play games with me!' He caught up with her in the hall and grasped her arm, swinging her to face him. 'You will leave Javier strictly alone, because this time I have no intention of dispatching you so rapidly. If my brother becomes attached to you, there will be trouble. Do not either try to turn *Abuela* from this. It is all arranged. Your friend will hire a car at the airport, and be here before it is dark. I have invited him to stay the night also.'

'I'm sure you're very kind!' Kate said sarcastically, removing her arm from his tight grip. 'Felix will be most impressed.'

'He is not required to be impressed, merely to confirm that you are to stay here and do the job!'

'Oh, he'll do that! He'll do anything I ask, in actual fact, and as I've decided to stay I certainly shall not be trying to turn *Abuela* from the idea.'

'I am most relieved,' he murmured caustically, his black brows drawn together in a very formidable scowl. 'The work will be better if you are not doing it while filled with resentment.'

'I assure you that the resentment I feel is all for you, and will remain constantly, but I'm well trained and very professional. I shall surprise you.'

'You already have,' he said smartly, his anger dying as humour and speculation took its place, and that was enough for her. She turned and walked off before he could see her red face. The memory of last night was written too clearly on Diego's face to be ignored. It was something that most certainly would not happen again. How it had happened she wasn't sure, and she didn't even want to think about it. One thing was certain—he had not felt her strange feeling of peace that even penetrated the harshly punishing kiss. It was one thing he didn't know about. She didn't even want to know about it herself.

Felix arrived in the late afternoon, and Kate was very glad to see him. Javier had gone off to the nearby town, inviting her along, but she had refused, her momentary desire to annoy Diego fading as the idea of the *sala grande* took shape in her mind. She was more concerned, too, with being on the spot when Felix arrived than with playing any games to annoy Diego. It would not have been a good idea to allow Diego any private words with Felix Merrol. He might find out things that she would rather he did not know.

She was right there when the hired car that brought Felix stopped in the courtyard. The tall frame unwound itself from behind the wheel and she greeted him somewhat effusively, to his obvious delight. In the first place it was wonderful to see him—dear, safe Felix. In the second place, if Diego was around she wanted to make him quite sure that his original estimation of her relationship with Felix was correct. She needed every advantage she could get with her so-called cousin.

'It's a long journey up here, Kate,' Felix muttered, his arm coming around her shoulders as they walked to the main doors. 'Well worth it, though. This is some place!'

His eyes roamed over the building, but she could see that he felt nothing that she had felt when she had first seen this place. To him, it was a very old house that needed attention, and his firm had the contract. That Kate was to do it was a bonus, but whatever his feelings he would be all businessman as he looked the place over.

Diego came to the door. Apparently he too had heard the car, and his eyes moved over the two of them—Kate flushed and smiling, Felix tall and fair, handsome in a very Anglo-Saxon way. His eyes returned to Kate, and she knew it was only with a great effort that he managed to be civil. He was probably wondering if she would change her mind and go off with Felix.

'Señor Merrol? I see that you have already been greeted. Let me offer you some refreshment, and then you can view the great *sala* and tell me your ideas.'

'Actually, the ideas will be Kate's,' Felix said later, as they all sat in the comfortable room next to the one that Kate was to work on. 'I'm only here to see she doesn't go overboard with expense—she sometimes gets a little too enthusiastic, don't you, darling?' he added, with a knowing smile at Kate that might have meant anything. It couldn't have been better, especially when he added, 'Of course, I wouldn't refuse the chance to be with her for a few hours either.' He took her hand and she began to wonder if she was being wise about this. She would never live it down when she went back to London.

Diego was not amused, however, and she felt a swift burst of fiendish pleasure as she noticed his forbidding frown. This was not at all businesslike! His dark eyes said so, and by the look of it he was blaming her entirely—not that it surprised her. He had decided exactly what she was like, and she was going out of her way to live up to it.

Felix had also made it quite clear who had the final word in this, and she did not suppose that Diego liked that either.

'Perhaps you should view the *sala* before the light goes totally,' Diego said tightly. 'You will want to see it with some daylight, I assume?'

'It's best, although I imagine Kate will already have given it some thought. She doesn't take long to reach conclusions.' Felix gave a little laugh. 'I expect you've realised that already?'

'It has not escaped my notice.'

Diego stood and led the way, and Felix made a wry grimace towards Kate.

'You've got a pretty tough cousin there,' he said in a low voice, and she couldn't correct him on the subject of relationship, as Diego was waiting at the door with ill-concealed impatience.

He did not accompany them, though. Instead he led the way and then left them to it, and they both soon forgot him as they began to assess the room and the usual arguments began.

'Well, I agree,' Felix said finally, his long, sensitive face rueful. 'And why I bother to go over things with you I don't know. You never give one inch!'

'Do I let you down?' Kate looked up at him and he smiled.

'No, Kate. You never let me down.' He looked at her for a minute, and then touched her cheek. 'What is it, Kate? Are you unhappy here?'

'Why do you say that?' she hedged, and he laughed softly.

'Because I know you, Kate. I probably know you better than anyone else does. Therefore I know you're not happy here.'

'No, I'm not happy here. It's nothing new.' She turned to walk up the long room, and he walked beside her, his arm across her shoulders.

'Say the word and I'll refuse the commission.'

That stopped her in her tracks and she stared up at him.

'Would you, Felix?'

'For you? Do you doubt it?' He looked worried and she smiled, her feelings at that moment real affection for him. She stood on tiptoe and kissed his cheek.

'This is a challenge, Felix, and I want to do it. I didn't, not until last night, but now I'm determined to do it. I have a debt to pay and a score to settle. One day, maybe, I'll tell you about it.'

'So long as you know what you're doing. So long as you're happy,' he said, giving her a hug.

It was at that moment that she saw Diego. He had come in with his usual silent tread, and she wondered how long he had been there. She hoped it was only long enough to see Felix hug her.

'You have reached an agreement?' Diego asked, as they both looked round to see him leaning elegantly by one of the long, dark tables.

'Not really. Kate decided,' Felix said with good humour. 'Perhaps you'd like to see what she's planned?'

'No. Whatever Kathryn decides I will agree to,' Diego said, astonishing Felix and making Kate look at him suspiciously.

'Well, there's a vote of confidence,' Felix murmured to Kate, and then added more seriously as Diego strolled towards them, 'Workmen will have to be found. We have our own in England, but as it's so far you'd probably like to find them here. Kate's not a painter and decorator, you know.'

'I am aware of it. I will arrange everything she needs. There is no language problem. She speaks my language fluently.'

'Oh, I know her little ways,' Felix said softly, glancing down at her, and right at that moment she didn't know which of them annoyed her most.

As they left the *sala* Kate wondered how she was going to fill in the rest of the afternoon. It was going to be with Felix, she was determined on that. His might be the only friendly male face she would see for a while, having burned her boats, as it were.

She hung back to speak to Diego as Felix stood in the hall and gazed about with the same entranced look on his face that had been on hers when she'd first come here.

'Felix is an expert on old chapels,' she said carefully. 'That's his great interest. May I show him the one here?'

Diego looked down at her from his tall, dark height. A strange look flickered across his aquiline face and then he smiled, a rather worrying smile.

'Need you ask? You may do anything. You live here.'

Annoyance and concern fought a battle on Kate's expressive face. She wasn't so sure of herself that she could ignore that tone.

'A temporary inconvenience,' she snapped quietly, and the dark eyes flashed with amusement.

'By all means, let us lower our voices and keep our battles private,' he murmured. 'I heard him say that he knew you best of all. Does he?'

Her skin flushed deeply and she looked away. 'It comes as no surprise to me that you listen to other people's conversations.'

'Surely it is necessary with you? It is the only way I am going to discover anything. For example, I now know that you are not happy. I also know that, in spite of his desire to introduce his firm into Spain, he will give it up for you.'

'I'm important to the firm,' Kate reminded him, but he looked at her sardonically.

'Not only to the firm, I would think.'

'Well, you knew that already, didn't you?' she asked tartly. 'Your previous foray into my private affairs gave you that bit of information.'

The dark eyebrows rose sceptically. 'You are a domineering female with a prickly disposition,' he murmured. 'I found that out too. You were not quite like that at seventeen.'

'How could I be anything else with you around?' she seethed in an equally low voice. 'It's the survival of the fittest. As to being seventeen, I was scared of you.'

'Only that?' He looked down at her mockingly. 'At least you do not make scenes in public,' he conceded, his voice merely a low growl. 'You differ from Lucia there. I suppose I should be thankful for that.'

'It's very easy to hate you!' Kate said bitterly.

'Is it?' His fingers trailed down her hot cheek, and then lingered against her suprised and parted lips. 'Run along and show your Englishman the chapel. I will still be here when he has gone. You may hate me then. You have all the time in the world.'

She didn't know if that was a threat or a promise. She almost ran to catch up with an unsuspecting Felix, scared because her lips were tingling.

Dinner promised to be a strain. Javier was back, his eyes narrowing as he looked at Felix, and Kate saw that this did not escape Diego's attention. There was a rather jealous look in Javier's eyes that threatened trouble in the future, and Kate began to wonder just what she had got herself into. Felix was amused. He was fairly astute himself.

'You're a rather unlikely relative,' he murmured. He looked at Javier and Diego, and then his eyes flashed over her hair. 'What did they make of your very un-Spanish appearance?'

'She is an oddity, but accepted with great joy. Her grandmother is delighted with her, and we are happy to have her back home at last.' Diego's remark, as he strolled over with his drink, brought Kate back to a state of nervous confusion, and she moved a little closer to Felix.

'That's true.' Javier came up too and she felt hemmed in. She was beginning to wonder if she would find that she was the one who had bitten off more than she could chew. Her plans didn't seem very clever now. Every time someone mentioned home she had an odd shivery feeling.

A flurry of sound by the door had them all spinning round, astonishment on almost every face. Ester was pushing the wheelchair into the room, a very determined Doña Elvira seated bolt upright in it.

The unexpected arrival silenced all conversation, and Ester wheeled her in, her expression saying that this was not her idea and that no good would come of it. Doña Elvira, though, had changed for dinner, her usual black discarded for a dark brown dress. There were brilliant jewels at her throat, and Kate felt a deep sense of pleasure at the sight of her. Her grandmother. It felt like it.

Liliana hurried over to her, but it seemed that Doña Elvira was in a party mood.

'Do not alarm yourself, Liliana,' the old voice said quite strongly. 'I have sent a message to the kitchen. We have a guest and I thought it best to be here for dinner. It will add a little excitement to my life. At dinner, I shall sit next to my *nieta*,' she finished happily, and Kate went across to her with a smile on her face.

'Should you be here, *Abuela*?' she asked quietly, and the old lady smiled like a mischievous girl.

'I expect not, but they would not dare to say so. I am too old to be chastised. This fact brings me many privileges.' She smiled up at Kate and they both laughed. 'Take my chair, and then I can dismiss Ester,' she whispered. 'She frowns all the time unless I am in bed. You may then introduce me to your handsome English friend.'

Kate exchanged a look of smiling understanding with Liliana and took charge, glancing up to find Diego watching her, his dark face quietly triumphant. It said everything to Kate. He had got his own way as usual. *Abuela* had her granddaughter, and it would be worth it even if that granddaughter ruined the great *sala*.

CHAPTER SIX

To KATE'S surprise, Diego invited Felix to stay until the necessary supplies were ordered and the workmen chosen. It suited her well. She normally did not have to search out workmen in England—the firm had their own. With Diego's directions and Kate's Spanish they managed, and when Felix left Kate started work on the *sala*. Diego would be away for several days, and during that time she would get on as fast as possible. Of course, everything relied upon the speed and efficiency of the workmen and the materials coming on time.

They did. During the afternoon a heavy lorry laboured its way to the *monasterio*, and she was soon in deep conversation with the people who would take away the fine old furniture and restore it to its previous glory. Like her, they were enthusiastic, running their hands lovingly over the old wood that had a sheen of silk about it even now.

No-sooner had they gone than the things she had ordered began to arrive, and Kate was kept very busy until dinnertime. Her lunch was served by one of the servants, and she ate it standing, her mind too busy with her work to take any time off.

It was only Liliana's entrance that slowed her down.

'You will make yourself ill if you intend to go on like this every day, Kathryn,' she said anxiously, and Kate stopped moving to smile across at her.

'Really I won't. When I get working I often eat on the run. I've survived so far.'

She felt cheerful today. With Diego out of the way, speeding northwards, she had at least a few days **of** respite.

'It looks barren without the furniture,' Liliana ventured, 'but then, it always looked barren. Apparently it was once very beautiful, but not in my time.' She looked thoughtful and then excited. 'Do you know, I believe there is furniture in the *áticos* that was once in this room. I have only been there once, and that many years ago, but as I recall it was very, very old.'

'And probably priceless,' Kate surmised excitedly. 'Can we look?'

The attics were at the very top of the *monasterio*, running along under the peaks of the towering roof-tops, and Kate was stunned at the treasures stored there so carelessly. She knew she would have to get the men back who restored furniture; already she could see it in her mind.

'It's so exciting!' she confided, as they at last returned to the hall. 'Just think of all that treasure up there!'

Impulsively she hugged Liliana, and Diego's mother smiled, her hand coming to Kate's arm. 'Who would have thought that one day Lucia's daughter would hug me?' she asked softly. 'It's wonderful to have you here, Kathryn.'

It left Kate with something to think about. How easily the two women here had accepted her. It was beginning to feel like home. She thought of Diego and shut the new idea firmly from her mind. She was always trying not to think of him at all.

Two days later the work was in full swing. The men arrived and at first were merely amused that a young and beautiful woman was in charge. They soon changed their minds. Kate's drive and expertise impressed even the most sceptical. Scaffolding went up, and within the first day the men were working furiously, driven by the same enthusiasm that lit Kate and extended to everyone who came into contact with her. She had seen it all before. It wasn't long before she was just one of the boys, and her fluent Spanish made conversation easy. They talked non-stop, but they worked all the time and she was well content with the progress.

Liliana came in as Kate was busily working while the men took their lunch-break, and she put her foot down.

'You must have a break,' she insisted. 'You will take lunch with me and get into the habit of a midday rest.'

Kate found it hard to stop when she was in her stride, but with a little coaxing Liliana got her to take the same amount of time off as the men and a new habit sprang up. Kate took her lunch with Diego's mother, and then sat with her in the garden until the workmen stirred and went back to the *sala*. It was refreshing, she had to admit that, and she knew that Liliana enjoyed it.

Javier arrived each night for dinner, and the meal was always enjoyable and friendly, laughter the norm. Kate was managing to keep him in his place, and she knew that Liliana approved. It would not be like that when Diego came back, and Kate found herself waiting with something that was more than anxiety for his return. There was not the same excitement in the air when he was absent, and her cheeks were warm when she admitted to herself that, in spite of their differences, she missed him.

Somehow *Abuela* was also fitted into her days. The old lady came for a few minutes each day to see the progress, and looked much more alert than she had done when Kate first arrived. Ester noticed it too, and her smile for Kate was one of warm approval. Each evening before dinner Kate went along to *Abuela's* suite and talked to her about anything that came into her head. It was good for everyone, it seemed, but whether it was good for herself Kate could only speculate about rather fearfully.

She had acquired a family she had not wanted, and she was getting very fond of them. She knew that, as far as the people here were concerned, she was welcome to stay forever. It was not, however, what she wanted. She told herself that very firmly.

The frescos on the high roof of the *sala* were being lovingly restored; the man working there was almost an artist in his own right. Kate deferred to him on most things, and watched each day the colours being restored to the brilliance that had once lit the whole roof.

'Señorita Hart!' he called down to her one afternoon. 'I cannot say that this colour pleases me. It appeared to be an exact match, but now that I see it close up and beside the other shades it does not look at all right.'

'The blue?' Kate looked upwards and shouted to him, her eyes on the high ceiling. From here it was impossible to tell. The pieces that finished stood out vividly, leaving the untouched places even more dim. 'I was a bit uneasy about that shade. Should we mix, do you think?'

'I would like your opinion, *señorita*. I am too close to the whole thing. A fresh eye is needed. Could you come up?'

It was a good excuse to get up there and have a close look. She had been wanting to do that for days. Heights never troubled her, and Kate was on the ladder at once, stepping from that to the scaffolding to stand beside the man and look long and hard at the work and the new colour. They could not afford to make a mistake. Hours of painstaking work would be ruined if the shade was out by anything at all.

'I agree. It's too deep. We'll have to mix. You'll never come up with that shade otherwise.'

'I can mix and try it on another part close by.' He lay down on the scaffolding to get a more panoramic view, and Kate did likewise, feeling a little like Michelangelo.

'You've done it beautifully!' she said excitedly, the incongruity of lying there beside the man and gazing upwards forgotten in her pleasure at the work already done. 'I'm going to leave it to you! You're the expert!'

'*Gracias,* Señorita Hart. You will not be disappointed,' he assured her in a pleased voice. 'I will begin with the paint I have, and then you must get more for me.'

Kate agreed and moved back to the ladder to make her way down, satisfied that he would do it well and that another firm ally had been secured. Satisfaction, pleasure and peace of mind left her with a sickening jolt as hard hands grasped her waist and lifted her from the ladder when she was a few feet from the bottom.

'Oh!' Her startled cry was the only sound that she was allowed to make as she was placed firmly on the floor, and then marched out of the *sala* so swiftly that her feet seemed to be almost touching air. 'You're back!' she gasped foolishly as she glanced in astonishment at Diego's furious face.

He didn't answer that inane remark. She was down the passage and inside his study before she really knew what was happening. He closed the door and swung her round, his eyes blazing.

'*Sí!* I am back! Back in time to see you lying down thirty feet in the air! Back in time to see you prancing down a swaying ladder with a sheer drop to stone flooring beneath you! In future you are forbidden to climb ladders and scaffolding!'

'I don't do as I'm told,' Kate retorted. 'Suggestions have a more lasting impression on me!'

'If you had fallen it would have killed *Abuela*!' he said furiously, and her eyes opened wide.

'Thank you very much! It wouldn't have done me a lot of good!' She pulled angrily away from his tight hold, pressing against the door to put some space between them. 'For your information, I do not make it a habit to stand back and admire work when I'm thirty feet in the air! As to *Abuela*, don't tell her! She'll sleep more easily if you keep it to yourself!'

'And how am I expected to sleep, knowing as I do that the moment my back is turned you become a circus act without the aid of a net?'

He suddenly looked unbearably harassed and Kate's temper slowly died.

'Look,' she said more softly, 'I've not been up there at all since you left. It was just that a colour was in question and the man asked me to take a close look. It is my responsibility, after all. With a bit of luck there's going to be no other time when climbing up there will be necessary.'

'See to it that there is not!' he commanded harshly, in no way softened by her reasonable tone. Her face tightened in annoyance and the soft tone left her immediately.

'I'll tell you what,' she suggested crossly. 'Just stop behaving like a big, domineering brother. Look upon me as just another workman!'

She moved to leave, turning away and feeling for the door-handle, but he grasped her shoulder, spinning her back to the hard wood of the door, his face taut, his eyes blazing.

'You are not a workman,' he rasped, 'even though you are dressed as one!' His dark eyes flared over her, from the dark blue jeans to the white shirt that she wore as a loose smock hanging over her belt. 'If you were a workman it would be quite suitable to have the buttons of your shirt unfastened, as you are woman it is not!'

Colour flared over Kate's face as she followed his eyes. More than the top button of her shirt was unfastened. Somehow in his angry dragging of her here the shirt had unfastened almost to her waist. The secret valley between her breasts was completely visible, the soft inner curve of each breast showing temptingly.

'I was quite decent until you started manhandling me,' Kate muttered, turning away rather desperately, her normally deft fingers fumbling with the buttons.

She was almost in tears. He could reduce her to raw feelings so quickly. Almost everything he said or did seemed to touch a nerve-ending, and to think that for a mad moment she had been glad to see him! She felt as self-conscious and vulnerable with Diego as she had done at seventeen. He could still hurt her feelings.

'Forgive me, Kathryn.'

The tone of his voice stunned her, and her fingers stilled as she kept her head firmly turned away, her fiery hair almost shielding her face. His hand touched her shoulder tentatively.

'With you, it seems, I do not know how to behave. I am not even civilised.'

Kate took a deep breath, unexpectedly shaken by his apology and his admission. 'I probably bring out the worst in you,' she murmured tremulously. 'I—I'm not the easiest person to get on with. I tend to go headlong into things.'

'And yet you have brought a great deal of happiness to your grandmother and to my mother.' His hand fell away and he moved back, giving her room. '*Abuela* seems to have taken on a new lease of life. I think the only thing that mars their joy is the fact that you will finally finish your task and go back to your own life in England.'

'I'll come back—to visit.'

She turned to look at him, her fingers still moving rather anxiously on the buttons of her shirt. Even though it was now securely fastened, she did not feel at all secure. There was an odd, frightening emptiness inside her, an emptiness that had never been there before—not even when her parents had died.

His dark eyes flashed to hers and held her gaze intently.

'For years *Abuela* has mourned for Lucia. You are here now, but for such a little time. I doubt if you can make up for the lost years. What is she to do? Is she to wait out her days hoping for a visit? It is not enough, but there is nothing that I can do about it.'

Tears came flooding unexpectedly to Kate's eyes, and she brushed them aside almost absently. She had never in her life questioned her mother's motives. She had felt a great deal of bitterness herself about this family. All the time they had been waiting to forgive, except perhaps Diego.

'I did not mean to make you cry,' he assured her quietly.

'It doesn't matter,' she got out in a painful voice. 'We brush each other up the wrong way. We just can't accept each other. It's a clash of character.'

She looked up and he was simply staring at her.

'I feel that you would be inclined to stay on a more permanent basis if I were not here.'

'No! No—I—I have a job in London, a place of my own, my own friends!'

He turned away impatiently and paced about. 'I find it hard to understand how it is that you are content to live in a small flat when you think on such a grand scale.'

'I only work with grand things. I can't afford to own them. Even to have a big flat I would have to share with someone else.'

'And you do not? What about Merrol?' His dark eyes held hers, and she blushed angrily, not really surprised that he thought badly of her.

'I don't know what you think of England, *señor*,' Kate said sharply, 'but we don't all live with a man. It's not exactly obligatory!'

He gave a soft, low laugh as a smile grew at the back of his eyes. 'I ask your forgiveness for my mistaken beliefs, and beg you not to call me by that unfriendly title.'

'It's self-defence,' she confessed blushingly, no longer able to meet the night-black eyes.

'Perhaps that is why I react so violently to you,' he suggested. 'We are defensive with each other.'

'Mutual dislike,' Kate muttered.

'I have not given any consideration to what else it might be,' he mused quietly.

Colour flooded into Kate's face, and her hands clenched tightly by her sides as waves of feeling washed over her. There was an intent look about him that both alarmed and excited her, and some great, leaping emotion hit her deep inside.

For a second her eyes looked deeply into his. He was so very different from her. There was nothing recognisable about him. He was so dark, so intense, and she looked at him helplessly, unable to free herself from his gaze until his eyes let her go, his power switched off at will.

'You are being called.' His voice was quiet as she simply stood on trembling legs and looked at him. It was only then that she heard one of the men calling, and she turned away quickly, almost missing the door-handle in her haste to leave.

She walked along the passage taking deep breaths to steady herself, almost back to normal as a smiling Spanish face informed her, 'Señorita Hart, I have the correct colour. Come and look.'

'No, thank you,' Kate said a little breathlessly. 'I believe you. I leave it all to you. I will not be climbing so high again!'

Nor falling into the same trap. What was Diego up to now? He had always disliked her, but he seemed to be almost willing her to look at him, his dark eyes hardly leaving her face when he was at home. She went to her room for a bath and a long, long think, although it didn't take much thought, and even less intelligence. She was acceptable now because *Abuela* was happy.

Kate had no alternative but to face Diego at dinnertime, and waves of anxiety hit her as soon as she saw him, because his eyes met hers immediately. It was a relief when *Abuela* was wheeled in.

It was Javier who hurried forward this time.

'Is this wise, *Abuelita*?' he asked, with the same smile that she invariably got from Diego.

'Perhaps not,' she answered with a smile of her own, 'but life has come to the *monasterio*. I now have something to look forward to each day. There is the great *sala* to inspect and there is my *nieta*.'

'When she goes home we will be desolate,' Javier said extravagantly, with a quick grin at Kate.

'It will be a long time before she goes,' Doña Elvira said comfortably, signalling Javier to manoeuvre her chair close to the table. 'The great *sala* will take some time. Later, perhaps she will decide to work on the chapel. There is a lot of room for improvement.'

Kate shot a look at Diego, but he was ready for her. He shook his head almost imperceptibly, his eyes cool at the fact that she had instantly suspected him of plotting yet again. There was something there, though, some deep look at the back of his eyes.

'When Kate leaves I will certainly miss her,' Liliana said. 'I may even go with her.'

Diego looked at Kate steadily, and then a smile edged his lips. 'Kathryn seems to be irreplaceable. She is also wearing herself out by working too hard, I hear.'

Kate's eyes flew to Liliana, and she shrugged, her hands held out helplessly.

'Believe me, Kathryn, I did not put it like that. I merely mentioned to Diego how hard you were working.'

'I always work flat out——' Kate said defensively, and Diego cut in in his usual sardonic manner.

'Then you will take a rest before you are indeed "flat out". Tomorrow I am going to the coast. I will take you with me.'

'I—I've got workmen here!' Kate protested, too astonished to make any real effort to get out of this.

'You will leave them with orders and take the day off——'

'Kate could come with me any day,' Javier interrupted, with a sullen look at his brother. It did nothing to unsettle Diego.

'She needs a rest. With you she would be taken from one nightspot to the other. Besides, I have seen her looking with great longing at the sea. Don't forget that in England the sea is all around her.' He dismissed Javier and turned his attention back to Kate. 'Well?' he asked imperiously.

'I—I . . . What am I supposed to say?'

She was unnervingly reminded of the time in the past when she had badly wanted to go with Diego.

'You are to say *muchas gracias* and accept graciously,' he informed her, his lips quirking.

Abuela found it very amusing, apparently. Liliana also had trouble holding in her laughter. Javier looked thoroughly disgusted, but, in any case, Diego ignored them all, his dark eyes amused and sardonic on her face.

'Thank you,' she said mutinously. 'I'll really try to be grateful.'

Abuela's black, intelligent eyes moved from one to the other, and Kate felt like hiding under the table. How did Diego manage to get her into these situations? She didn't want to be taken to the seaside like a child! He had no idea how to treat her.

Even so, she left with Diego fairly early in the morning after a flurry of worried questions from the men, who had by now come to accept her and rely on her judgement. Diego waited patiently, his face for once not showing the sardonic expression she was used to.

'I hope you're not going to regret this,' she said a little tersely as they drove off.

'Regret it? You intend to be troublesome?' His dark eyes flashed to her and she frowned.

'I was speaking about the workmen. Suppose something goes wrong?'

'What can go wrong? If something does, then they will correct it and I will be paying for it. You worry needlessly.'

'I do not!' Kate snapped. 'Money can't help, either, if something really priceless is spoiled.'

'You are too much of a perfectionist,' he murmured. 'Forget buildings and concentrate on people for a change.'

'I prefer buildings,' she said waspishly. 'They just don't say anything.'

'If we are to fight all day, then you will have gained nothing from your rest,' he murmured. 'We had better agree now to say as little as possible to each other.'

'I don't know why you bothered to bring me,' Kate fretted, and he smiled ironically, his eyes on the twisting road.

'Perhaps I wish to know how it is that you are able to charm my mother, my brother and *Abuela*, and merely battle with me. There must be something that I am missing.'

'Have you given any thought to the fact that you're not like the others?' Kate asked tartly. She closed her eyes and leaned back, the sunlight on her face, determined to say nothing more.

'Have you?' he asked softly.

She kept her eyes tightly shut, ignoring the quiet, dark voice and regretting this trip. She should have insisted on staying. She should have insisted on staying in England too, but he had managed to get her here, and it was a little too late now because she was becoming very fond of *Abuela* and Liliana. As to Diego, she just dared not think about him too deeply, although he seemed to walk into her every thought. It was better to go on fighting.

The run to the sea was longer than she had imagined. From the heights that surrounded the *monasterio* the sea had seemed almost close, but she had forgotten the steeply winding road. She had forgotten it easily, and she stared at the landscape, not really seeing it at all when she also realised that she had forgotten London and her life there. She seemed to have been here forever, the way they had easily seeped into her life.

Working on the great *sala*, too, was not like any task she had undertaken before. She was just a little too committed to it, as if it belonged to her. She had begun to think of it as home, of the Alvarez family as her own.

Her eyes looked stealthily at Diego. There was that strange, daunting air of power about him, even though he was sitting at ease, driving her to the sea. She felt like a very young girl again. She had never met a man like him before, or since, and she supposed she had been spoilt. There was nothing that the men in her particular sphere could do that she could not do as well or better, and she had never before had this feeling that she had met her match, someone who could easily master her, someone to lean on.

The tight, breathless feeling came back and she sat up straight, frightened when she remembered that he only had to reach across and touch her and she would be calm again. His eyes flickered to her and she hastily looked away.

'You seem to have little curiosity today,' he remarked quietly. 'Do you not wish to know where I am taking you?'

'To the sea,' Kate said, turning her head away. 'In England it's enough to be told that you're going to the sea if you're a child, and that's how you're treating me, isn't it?'

'Such antagonism,' he chided mockingly. 'I have been speaking to my mother and I am forcing you to take a rest. After all, it is my fault that you are here. I would not want you to work yourself into any state of ill-health in order to finish quickly and be done with us.'

'I'm not doing that,' Kate said breathlessly. 'I'm just interested, that's all.'

'A day away from it will merely sharpen your interest. It will also ease my conscience.'

'You have one?' Kate murmured ironically.

'Sometimes.' He shrugged and dismissed the subject, taking up another she would have liked to avoid. 'Have you been ill?'

'No. Just unhappy.' Kate kept her answer very short, her voice guarded, but he persisted.

'From time to time you are very pale. The work on the *sala* can wait. Why not rest and take it up later?'

'There's no "later",' Kate assured him. 'I work in England. This is merely a job, and when it's finished I'll go back.'

'You will be glad to leave Spain?' he asked softly. '*Abuela*, then, has not touched your heart?'

'Too much,' Kate said almost bitterly. 'You knew she would. I like your mother too, and Javier,' she added deliberately, leaving out any mention of Diego, and his lips quirked as he answered.

'You have gained a family, *señorita*, even though one member of it is not to your liking. You will find it very difficult to leave.'

'Are you threatening me?' Kate spun round to glare at him, tension mounting inside her, but he didn't even look at her; his dark eyes were on the road that fell towards the sea.

'I do not make threats, Kathryn. I make promises.'

There was something about the dark voice that made her continue to gaze at him, and for a moment he turned his head, his eyes meeting hers before he turned back to the road, leaving her with only the sight of his cool, arrogant profile.

They drove through a fishing village and Diego stopped at a small shop, coming out after a few minutes with various bags under his arm, that he put into the back of the car before driving on until the village was out of sight.

The coast was rugged, and here by the sea it was gloriously hot. Kate wanted to stretch like a cat in the sunshine, and her eyes were held by the blue and green glitter of the water. She wanted to get out, but she refused to ask him to stop. He seemed to know how she felt, though, because he said quietly, 'Round the next headland we will stop and park the car. You may then go into the sea.'

His patronising tone stung her and she answered sharply.

'Just a look at it will be enough. In any case, I've not brought a swimsuit.'

'I brought one for you—knowing your contrary mind,' he said smoothly. 'I had a maid get one from your room this morning, and don't ask me how "I dare",' he added as she opened her mouth to do that. 'I have become quite accustomed to the fact that you are prepared to suffer discomfort rather than be gracious.'

It made her feel like an uncouth ten-year-old, and she swore silently not to wear the swimsuit or even dabble her toes. Her resolution faded, though, when she saw the bay where he stopped the car. It was a great arc of clear, blue water, surrounded by towering headlands, and so quiet that she knew there was nobody else for miles.

'This is as far as we go by car,' he said, getting out and collecting the bags. 'Now we walk down.' He went to the boot and took out a roll of towels, tossing them to her. 'You will carry this. I will carry the lunch.'

The bags apparently contained the lunch, and she was a bit surprised. It would have been more in keeping with Diego to stop at some grand hotel. It just showed, you never knew people, unless he thought she might make a scene and embarrass him?

'Your swimwear is in the towels,' he informed her derisively. 'I am wearing mine.'

'You expect me to change on the beach?' she enquired crossly, and the black eyebrows shot up with surprised mockery.

'Not unless you feel the need to. There is a cave. Come along, now. You may intend to sulk all day, but I intend to swim.'

He held out his hand, but she ignored it, quite sure that she could manage the rather steep descent alone. She was glad to accept his help, though, when she seemed to make a flying start, and only his strong brown hand prevented her from reaching the beach well before him by rolling down the whole way. She was quite disconcerted when he made no comment, but after a second the picture of herself rolling in an ungainly manner down the steep hill made her smile, and he glanced at her in amusement.

'Having a cousin is somewhat of a trial,' he murmured. 'I shall never search the world for another.'

'Don't worry. I'll be gone soon enough,' she said pertly, a little shocked when this thought now brought no comfort at all. Her teeth bit into her lip and she was grateful when he sighed mockingly.

'You intend to spoil my day, I presume? I will have to dump you in the sea.'

As it turned out there was a small cave, almost nothing more than an indentation made by the sea into the hard rock-face, but it was sufficient to give privacy. Diego put the bags in the entrance and left her to decide for herself whether she would swim or sulk. Kate sat down and stared at the sea, and presently she saw him go down the beach, his clothes discarded on the sand, his brief black shorts showing strong brown legs.

When he waded out and then dived into the clear water she could not sit still any longer. She changed as quickly as possible, pressing herself uncomfortably against the cave wall for further privacy, and then running down the sand to the sea before he could come out and watch her.

Apparently he was in a mood to be playful, a thing she had never suspected him capable of, because he surfaced close to her and advanced so threateningly that she gave a little shriek and turned to swim away quickly. A few powerful strokes caught her, and she found herself looking into two glittering eyes, his teeth white against the dark, wet bronze of his face as he took her shoulders and forced her beneath the water.

Kate panicked and her hands reached out frantically for help, her searching fingers encountering the smooth power of his chest and reaching for his shoulders to pull herself out of the water. She was instantly free, lifted above the waves as he took her by the waist and hoisted her into the air, looking up into her rather desperate face.

'You are afraid of me? If I wish to be rid of you, I will not resort to violence.' For a moment he held her by the waist, his hands lightly gripping her as he looked into her eyes. He seemed to see the way that panic left her, just as his touch had drained her feeling of tension more than once, and she tried to look away, with very little success.

'I don't understand you.' Her voice was almost plaintive, fretful, and he smiled one of his worrying smiles as he let her feet touch the sandy bottom of the bay.

'You expect to? You are too deeply concerned with battle to even begin to understand me. I strongly suspect that you do not even understand yourself.'

'I do. I know exactly where I'm going—what I'm going to do with my life.'

He nodded, irony twisting his lips. 'You are going to prove yourself to be as good as the next man? Is this the only passion your mother left you?' She tossed her hair back from her face angrily, and he suddenly stroked it away, his fingers in the wet strands. 'I cannot make up my mind whether you are to be pitied or blamed, whether you should be shaken or soothed.'

'I'm not a wayward child!'

He glanced over her with soft mockery, his glittering gaze skimming her bikini-clad figure. 'Perhaps you should let your mind grow to match your body, then,' he suggested softly. 'Bright intelligence does not necessarily prepare you for life—in its sweeter forms.'

'Life is sweet to me,' Kate said a little desperately, and he smiled slowly.

'Is it?' He pulled her against him until there was no water swirling between them, until her legs were tightly against his. 'Is it sweet enough, Kathryn?'

CHAPTER SEVEN

DIEGO let Kate go, and moved away from her with powerful strokes, and she watched his dark head in the water, his brown arms cutting through the waves. She was back to her first statement. She didn't understand him. She fought him because she was apprehensive when he was there, unsure of herself for the first time ever. When he touched her it was like fire, a wild surge of power that threatened to fuse her to him. It drained her anxiety, made her safe, and excited her in a way she had never known before.

She turned away, irritation washing over her as strongly as the waves. What was she thinking of? He had come back into her life like a tiger, demanding and arrogant. Now he was playing some game of his own— no doubt with *Abuela's* happiness in mind. Kate was happy enough in England with her job. He didn't know her at all, and she was a lot safer not knowing him.

Kate walked out of the sea and began to make her way to the cave, startled when out of a clear blue sky heavy rain began to fall. It was so sudden, so heavy that she made a run for the shelter of the cave, some kindly instinct making her snatch up Diego's clothes en route. Left out there they would be soaked, and she had a feeling of a good deed done as she raced to the cave and sank down inside, her eyes on the rain that lashed across the beach.

Diego didn't come. At first she thought he had decided to stay in the water as he was already wet, but as

117

the time passed and he still did not appear she became anxious, finally venturing outside to look as best she could to where the waves were now white and not nearly so friendly-looking. She had heard that storms could come from nowhere in the Mediterranean, and although there was no thunder it was a really strong rainstorm, the sea now not at all safe. She stood in the pouring rain, not knowing what to do, frightened for him, a growing dread in her mind.

He appeared from nowhere, taking her arm and urging her back into the shelter of the cave before she had quite realised he was safe.

'Where have you been?' She turned on him resentfully, her anger a shield to hide the growing again of the breathless tension and her relief to see him.

'I might say the same thing to you. I have, in fact, been looking for you.'

He hadn't. He wouldn't bother.

'You mean you didn't think I had the sense to come in out of the rain?'

'Perhaps.' He began to dry himself with a calm air about him that made her feel worse, and she turned away, her shoulders tight.

'You're impossible! It's no use trying with you, is it? For all I knew you might have been——'.

'You feared for me? You sound like a scolding wife. Does this mean that my fiery cousin has a soft place in her heart, even for me?'

'It means that I was wondering how I was going to get back to the *monasterio* if you drowned,' she said tartly, hiding behind sharp words. 'You'll notice I collected your clothes. I had the presence of mind to realise that the car keys would be in your pocket.'

'I did not drown. You can relax.' He draped a dry towel over her shoulders, his hands holding it there. 'Get dry and change,' he suggested softly. 'There is no need to be so edgy, Kathryn.'

She stood still, almost unable to breathe, and he turned her slowly, his dark eyes searching her face. 'You assured me that you were not ill,' he reminded her quietly, 'but you are trembling, pale, and very obviously distressed—even your ready tongue cannot hide that. You know I am too strong to be defeated by a few heavy waves, so what is it?'

Kate looked down and shook her head.

'Sometimes—sometimes,' she began tremulously, 'I can't... Since the funeral...I...'

She had no idea why she was telling him—Diego, of all people—but she came unresistingly when he drew her forward. His arm came around her, his other hand soothing against her nape, his fingers pushing aside her wet hair as he pulled her head to his shoulder.

'And I make matters worse?' He tilted her face, looking down at her, but she shook her head.

'Not really. It just happens and I can't fight my way out of it. When you touch me——'

She stopped, appalled at her admission, at the words that had so readily come to her tongue, and he looked at her intently before his hand slid around her face, his other arm drawing her closer.

'When I touch you it all goes away.' He smiled at her confusion. 'It is no secret. I already know this. It has happened to you before, and I am not altogether stupid. I can feel the tension leaving you. Perhaps I have the magic touch?'

Her ready tongue was useless. Her bones seemed to be melting, and when his lips closed over hers she didn't do a single thing to resist him. Her whole body seemed to relax, to rejoice in a very strange sort of peace. How peculiar that this man who was power and arrogance should be able to turn her to such tranquillity. He was forceful, fierce, his whole character explosive, and yet she was languorous in his arms, passive, as if the whole world were being held in abeyance.

He raised his head and looked at her, but she made no effort to move as he searched for her lips again, his arms tightening even further around her, and when he let her go she was stunned by the feeling of loss. She resented it that his lips were not on her own, and it was cold without his arms around her.

'Get dried and put on your clothes,' he murmured. 'The medical assistance is over as the patient has apparently recovered. I would not wish to generate a more serious condition.'

His voice was softly taunting, and Kate turned away abruptly, snatching a towel that had fallen to the floor.

'I can hardly put on my clothes with you here,' she managed shakily. Her arms had been tightly around his neck and she had only just realised it.

'We will turn our backs to each other. I promise not to look.'

It was all very embarrassing, and she didn't want to turn even when she was dressed. She was afraid to meet those dark, mocking eyes, because now he had a decided advantage. He could make her melt and he knew it. She could still feel his arms around her, and it was frightening to feel so dazed and lost.

He was opening the bags when she turned, and he handed her some lunch. The coffee was still hot, and he pointed out that the containers were specially prepared for this sort of picnic.

'I did not intend that you should spend an afternoon in a cave,' he murmured ruefully as they sat and ate, watching the rain and the now rather wild sea. 'Sometimes the rains and storms come quite unexpectedly in these parts. It is a little early in the season, though. Perhaps we are going to have bad storms this year.'

She knew he was speaking in this matter-of-fact voice to ease the embarrassment she felt, and an odd feeling of gratitude swept over her.

'Thank you for—for...'

'Kissing you?' he enquired softly. 'My pleasure, *señorita*. Any time. It is quite safe with you, I think. There is little chance of any misplaced passion as you dislike me so roundly. You are not likely to be overwhelmed by your own desires, as was your mother. Besides, there is Merrol, is there not?'

'Yes,' Kate snapped bitterly, hurt by the softly taunting voice. 'I'm not likely to forget Felix!'

'You think not?' He deliberately placed his coffee down, reaching for her when she began to move hastily away, a devil roused in his dark eyes. 'Let us see.' His arms closed round her and he pushed her to the sandy floor of the cave, the weight of his body subduing her instant struggles.

'Now, firebird, tell me about Merrol.'

He took her face between his hands and began to kiss her slowly and deeply until her whole body trembled. His lips moved from hers to her eyes, her cheeks, her neck, and there was no resistance in her at all when his hand cupped her breast and his lips covered hers again in one long kiss, as his fingers stroked her soothingly and rhythmically.

When he let her go she was almost sobbing with panic at the feelings she had been forced to fight, and he looked at her for a long moment.

'The body is willing but the mind is not,' he remarked astutely, only a flare of colour across his cheekbones to show he had not been entirely unmoved himself. He pulled her up to a sitting position, but she scrambled shakily to her feet, terrified to look at him and show how defenceless she was when he held her.

'Can we go, do you think?' she asked, standing and facing the open, where the rain had now slowed to a very thin drizzle. 'As you say, a cave is not much fun.'

'It could be,' he murmured sardonically, 'if one had the right companion. Unfortunately, we are stuck with each other, and I agree, it is not much fun. You no doubt find more excitement instructing the workmen.'

'Definitely!' Kate affirmed tightly, scooping up the towels and stepping out into the wet afternoon.

The whole expedition had been a very big mistake. She was trembling, scared as she had never been before by the feelings inside her, and as she had to sit in the car and wait as he called at various places on the way back, including a farm where a very pretty girl came to the gate with him to see him off, her eyes lingering on him longingly, Kate vowed that in future Javier would be given the privilege of escorting her. She was old enough to deal with Javier now. Diego had left her feeling vulnerable, and she didn't like that. She didn't like the way her mind kept going back to the feel of his arms around her, either, or his lips on hers. More than anything, though, she didn't like the sardonic look on his face. He seemed to think he had scored a point in a battle for supremacy. She was more than ever determined to finish the *sala grande* and go back to England quickly.

When they got back there were visitors. Kate would have liked to escape instantly to her room, but it was not an easy task with Diego's hand like steel on her arm. She felt utterly unkempt, and she was perfectly sure that he knew how she felt and was intent on making her face strangers in that state. Her hair, normally unruly, was now perfectly wild. The sea and the rain had left it a mass of red-gold curls that cascaded round her head and fell to her shoulders, and Diego's fingers in her hair had made things even worse. Her clothes, too, left much to be desired. They had been flung down in the cave and then donned hurriedly, and it was not with a feeling of being band-box fresh that she entered the smaller *sala* and met the visitors.

They were a brother and sister, Cristina and Enrique Serrano, and from the way that the girl greeted Diego Kate thought that a minor mystery had been solved. The woman in his life was obviously here, and was greeted almost tenderly for such a powerfully arrogant man.

The girl was small and dark, her vivacious face turned with deep interest towards Kate.

'Your cousin, Diego?' she said sweetly. 'We met Javier today and he was full of praise for his new cousin. We had to come and see for ourselves, didn't we, *querido*?' she asked her brother.

'Indeed. It is no disappointment either.' His dark eyes roamed over Kate with a boldness that annoyed her and brought a quick frown to Liliana's pleasant face.

'We are very fond of Kathryn,' she said, with more force than she usually used. '*Abuela* is devoted to her.'

There was an edge of warning in her voice that told them that if they were to remain welcome here they had better not overstep the mark with this new cousin. Kate was grateful, and made her excuses to leave before coffee was served. She had no intention of being there under Diego's sardonic gaze and watching the girl preen for him. As to Enrique, he was just a little too forward to her way of thinking. She hurried to her room for a bath and to wash her hair, staying there as long as possible, and only coming down when it was clear that dinner would soon be served.

Diego pounced on her as she entered the *sala*.

'I do not expect normality from Lucia's daughter,' he rasped quietly. 'However, courtesy would be nice. Knowing that we have guests, you have deliberately stayed in your room.'

'They're not my guests,' Kate bit out quietly. Now that she was changed, her hair once again a glorious, shining mass of waves and curls, her cream dress swirling around her calves and clinging to her in all the right places, she was back to her normal self and quite ready to do battle, especially as he had kissed her like that with this girl here waiting for him impatiently.

'You live here. Therefore you are expected to be here when guests arrive.'

'I do not live here and I do exactly as I like——' she began heatedly, her face flushing when he took her arm and led her forward with a few whispered words.

'I will not argue with you. It would be difficult if your breathlessness returned and you needed to be kissed. Cristina would never believe the explanation.'

There was nothing at all she could say to defend herself, and she greeted Javier with an almost hysterical relief when he came across and rescued her. A wolf was easier to cope with than a tiger.

'I hear that you are painting the *sala grande*?' Cristina said rather disdainfully as they ate. 'This is what you do for a living?'

'Yes, I'm a painter and decorator——' Kate said brightly, getting ready to expand on this theme when Diego cut in smartly.

'She is no such thing,' he informed the two with a subduing look at Kate. 'Kathryn is an interior designer. She is the star attraction of one of the most prestigious firms in England. She has been—loaned to us,' he added with a scathing look at Kate.

'How long will it take?' Cristina asked, with no smile at all, and Kate looked back pleasantly.

'Not too long. I have too much waiting for me in England for any lingering. Of course,' she couldn't help adding, 'I shall be coming back regularly. According to Diego, I'm needed here.'

'You are needed here according to everyone,' Javier said firmly, his hand on hers. 'And speaking of needing, will you go to the city with me tomorrow evening? You were with Diego today and I feel that it is my turn now.'

'You have been out with your cousin today?' Cristina asked with a sharp look at Diego.

'We had a picnic in a cave,' he said with a sardonic glance at Kate. 'It was a very interesting time, a good way to get to know someone.'

What he had intended by that remark Kate did not know, but its effect was electric. Every eye turned on her, and she found herself blushing helplessly, Diego watching her with as much attention as everyone else. She couldn't wait to escape, and later as she made her way to her room she met Diego in the passage below the stairs.

'How dare you embarrass me like that?' she stormed quietly.

'Embarrass you? I spoke only the truth.' He put his head on one side and looked at her tauntingly. 'I have said that it is good that you do not make scenes in public, but perhaps it would be less of a strain on you if you did. Suppressed anger can only bring on another attack of tension, and then I would have to help you out again. It would be difficult here on the passage.'

'You're hateful!' Kate snapped, and he smiled derisively.

'Cristina does not think so, but never mind, little cousin. Tomorrow I am leaving the *monasterio* for a few days. You will be able to manage better without me, I think.'

'I certainly will!' Kate snapped, swirling away and leaving him once again looking after her as she went up the long stairs.

Diego went off next day to the south coast, to Malaga where the Alvarez family had a great deal of property, and Kate was glad not to have the need to be constantly facing him. Javier stayed at home much more, and Kate suspected that with *Abuela* so old there was an arrangement whereby one or other of them should be on hand. Javier did not take his duties quite as seriously as his older brother did, and Kate was invited out almost every night. She declined. She was working hard and was often tired, but, more than that, she did not want to be more than a very distant relative to Javier. His constant attention was a little worrying, and she knew it annoyed Diego. She had enough trouble without any other sort adding itself to things. She didn't want to have to put him down severely, because under it all he was nice enough, and she had promised *Abuela* that she would come back to Spain regularly.

Daily the great *sala* became more beautiful and, as the effect became more obvious, the enthusiasm of the workmen grew. Liliana spent a great deal of time watching and talking to Kate when work was not too overwhelming, and she was always there at lunchtime to see that Kate had some time off to relax in the gardens. *Abuela* sometimes joined them, and more and more each day Kate became a part of the family she had not wanted at all.

She really had no desire whatsoever to leave the *monasterio*, but one morning she was faced with a halt to a part of the work unless she made a journey for the paint needed to mix for the frescos. Javier had already left, and there was nothing for it but to go to the city herself. It worried Liliana.

'You can take one of the cars, Kathryn, but it's not an easy journey until you get out of the mountains. It looks like rain too.'

Kate was both amused and touched by this concern. 'I'm used to driving in London,' she said with a smile. 'As to the mountains, I'll be very careful. A little rain isn't going to worry me.'

'It may not be just a little, Kathryn. The rains are due, and when they come we can get severe storms here. The mountain roads are then very dangerous. I shall be most anxious until you get back.'

Kate hesitated for a moment. She had no desire to worry anyone, least of all Liliana, but she did not have the nature that would wait patiently and she wanted to see the ceiling finished and in its old glory. If she would admit it, which she would not, she wanted it finished before Diego returned. It had become foolishly important to her that he approved.

She almost shook herself. Even if he did approve, he would never say so, and why should she care anyway?

'I'll get off and be back in no time at all,' she said cheerfully. 'Did you say I could take one of the cars?'

'Of course, though what Diego will say——'

'He'll object to one of his cars being borrowed?' Kate began rather hotly, but Liliana shook her head.

'If he objects, it will be because I have allowed you to risk your life.' Kate was stunned, until she remembered his words when he had stormed at her for climbing the scaffolding. It would worry *Abuela*. *That* would be the source of Diego's objection.

She was still musing about that as she carefully negotiated the mountain road. In any case, the sky was blue, the sun hot, and she could not imagine a storm coming from this lovely day. As to Diego, if he objected it would be merely because he was grasping every chance to get at her. He wouldn't even know, anyway.

It was easy when she reached the main road, and the city when she came to it was oddly familiar, the suppliers she and Felix had used easy to find. She hardly seemed to have been away at all, and she parked the car and spent some time looking at the shops, buying herself a new dress for dinner and some lovely shoes.

By the time she turned for home it was later than she had intended, and beginning to get dark, but she would be back for dinner, and the next day the frescos could be continued with no further need to wait.

Darkness came rapidly, not only with the uncanny speed that brought evening to this part of Spain, but because the sky was beginning to darken rather ominously with more than approaching night. Rain began to fall long before she had reached the mountain road, and as she began the long, dangerous climb to the *monasterio* Liliana's words were at the very top of her mind.

It was almost impossible to see, the rain altogether too much for the wipers even when they were going at top speed. Every anxious glance to the side of the road showed her that water was coming in increasing torrents from the higher mountain peaks. It left the trees and came across the uneven road in great tides of muddy brown like so many rivers in flood.

Kate began to think of rock-falls, thankful for the protection of the trees. There was thunder but no lightning, and the noise of water drowned out the sound of the car's engine altogether. She began to understand Liliana's fears. She was afraid herself, the *monasterio* a refuge she prayed for with urgency.

Suddenly there was a great splintering crash, and, with no warning other than the sound, a tree fell across the road, making her jam on the brakes, the nose of the car almost touching the tree. It frightened her more than anything else could have done. She was still a long way from the *monasterio*, not even at the small village, and she was stranded.

She got out into the pouring rain that immediately drenched her to the skin, making her skirt and blouse cling to her uncomfortably. The headlights showed her the impossibility of trying to go further. The tree was completely blocking the road and, although it was by no means a giant of a tree, it looked too heavy to move. She had to try, though. She stepped into the lights and began to push at the tree, knowing perfectly well that it was all useless effort.

Kate was so absorbed, tears of frustration on her wet face, that she never saw the lights coming towards her from the direction of the *monasterio*, and it was not until she was flooded with further illumination that she lifted her head, pushing the long wet hair back from her face. She had no time to speak, though, because Diego's voice came over the noise of the rain and thunder.

'Kate! Come here!'

He came towards her quickly, and she could see him in the lights of both cars, his jacket soaked already.

'I can't move the tree. Help me to——'

'Come to me, Kate! *Now!*'

The urgency of his voice penetrated her mind and she moved towards him, gasping with shock when he leaned forward and lifted her over the tree, not letting her go until he had almost thrown her into his car. She was so stunned that she could not manage a word until she realised he was reversing rapidly, dangerously to her way of thinking.

'The car! Can't we move the tree with——?'

He reversed into a clearing to turn his car, the wheels spinning in the mud, and then she heard the sound she had been subconsciously dreading: the great roar of falling earth and rocks. As they turned, her eyes watched in horror the headlights of her borrowed car lifting crazily into the air as it was swept from the path like some matchwood toy, rolling down the mountain with the tree and others, a terrifying volume of muddy water and rocks forcing it away with vicious ease.

Diego spun on to the road and raced for safety, and she gripped the seat in fear, her wet state forgotten as the whole mountain seemed to be coming down, chasing them.

He didn't speak. Even when the danger was past and the *monasterio* in sight, he grimly held the silence. She seemed to be incapable of speech herself. All she was able to think of was that the paint was lost, and that Diego had called her Kate. He could have been killed. She dared not even look at him.

The *monasterio* seemed to be in a minor upheaval, and Liliana took one look at Kate and led her firmly up the stairs, her wet clothes trailing water every step.

'There was a landslide,' she managed through trembling lips as Liliana ran a hot bath and began to remove her wet clothes with a grim determination.

'A flash-flood,' she said quietly. 'It is exactly what I feared.'

'I'm sorry, Liliana. Diego could have been killed.'

'He did not give much thought to that. His concern was for you.' Liliana sounded angry and Kate burst into tears, at last giving way to the terror and her deep feeling of guilt. Liliana was instantly contrite, her arm coming around Kate's shaking shoulders.

'There now,' she said soothingly. 'We were all afraid for you. Anxiety shows itself in many ways. Diego has gone to change and then assure *Abuela* that you are all right. After that I expect you will have to face him.'

'What—what will he say?' Kate asked foolishly, all her desire for battle and supremacy gone.

'I dare not think,' Liliana murmured, back to her smiling self. 'He can be very daunting. Your only chance is to look helpless. Into your bath, Kathryn. Call if you need me, otherwise I will see you at dinner. I will leave you to practise a defenceless expression.'

It didn't do her a bit of good. She was sitting in her robe, drinking hot tea that a servant had brought at Liliana's orders, her hair a tangled mass of wet curls, her eyes still haunted by the fright, when Diego simply walked in without any pretence of knocking.

His eyes swept over her angrily as he advanced, and she stood quickly, vaguely thinking about making a dive for the bathroom and safety. He didn't say a word, and Kate felt she had about one second to get her excuses in. He looked wild enough to shake her violently.

'I—I'm sorry,' she began hastily. 'I'm sorry about the danger you were in and the car and——'

'What about the anxiety you have caused my mother and *Abuela*?' he rasped.

'It was sunny, warm, I didn't realise that... I needed paint...'

'And where is your paint now?' he roared, no thought whatsoever for the noise he was making, or the panic that was spreading across her face.

'It's—it's gone,' she gulped.

'Gone where the car has gone! Gone where you too may have gone so easily!' He grasped her shoulders, jerking her towards him. 'You are so determined to have your own way in all things, so exactly like Lucia!'

'I'm not! She wasn't like me. She was gentle and kind and——'

'Ah! So you are admitting that you are not? You agree that you wish to fight all comers, to be the best man present?'

'I've told you I'm sorry,' she managed, tears coming back when she least wanted them. 'I just didn't understand that——'

'You mean that you were not prepared to listen or be advised!' he grated, interrupting her again.

'I've never been in such a country,' she snapped, tears running down her cheeks as she looked up at him resentfully. He was as hard as nails, and he didn't care at all that she was shaking and upset. 'I couldn't begin to envisage what might happen. I'll pay for the dammed car!'

It seemed to be the thing to drive him really over the top. His grip tightened and he actually lifted her off her feet, his fingers digging painfully into her slender shoulders.

'You dare to suggest that I am anxious about a car?' he thundered. 'Your life hung by a single thread of time, and you insult me by offering to pay for a piece of metal?'

'Why not?' Kate asked tearfully, too scared to keep quiet. 'I'm not really your cousin. I'm nothing to you.'

'Oh, yes, you are,' he ground out menacingly. 'You are a daily irritation, a fiery opponent I could well do without. You are prickly and domineering, hiding your femininity behind a masculine skill and a tongue like a knife. Your stupidity is boundless—bordering on the supernatural—and my own must be similar or I would never have manoeuvred you into staying here.'

Kate cringed for the first time in her life. His anger and his words hurt; they hurt much more than the tight grip he kept on her arms, and new tears flooded into her eyes and hung there like diamonds, the deep blue shining through almost blindingly.

His grip eased as he gazed at her and almost absently his fingers soothed the places he had almost burned with tight fingers.

'Are you now using those feminine wiles you mentioned?' he murmured. 'Is this how you succeed when all else fails? You look at me with tear-filled blue eyes and stand crushed and defeated. Am I supposed to feel pity, to respond to this soul-stirring gaze?'

'I'm never crushed,' Kate said in a tremulous voice, 'and I don't suppose you ever feel anything.'

'You suppose wrongly,' he murmured, pulling her closer. 'I feel fear, as much as the next man, when I see you standing wet and helpless and half a mountain ready to fall on you. The car and your paint are over the edge of the mountain, buried in hard rock and mud. At any moment you also——'

'Don't! Please don't!'

Kate hid her face in her hands and his arms lashed around her as he held her closely, his face against her wet cheeks.

'Stop crying, Kate,' he said thickly. 'The *monasterio* has stood here impregnable for longer than anyone can remember. You are safe, and even if the grand *sala* has to be finished in red enamel you will never again go to the city alone.'

She looked up at the tight sound of his voice and he caught her lips in a deep and probing kiss, his hand cupping her wet hair as his lips searched hers for endless minutes.

Peace flooded through her, and an excitement that rose above her common sense. When he lifted his head she could only look up at him in a daze, and his dark eyes held hers for a second.

'Why—why did you do that?' she asked shakily, foolishly hoping he would say that he cared about her. Not Diego.

'I imagined that I had driven you to a state of tension,' he said mockingly, his dark gaze showing no emotion. 'I already seem to have taken on the duty of easing your distress. This time I thought it a good idea to act first before necessity drove you to beg.'

Kate turned away in confusion before he could see that she wanted to beg now, to beg to be right back in the arms that had readily released her.

'I—I suppose *Abuela* has been worried?' she said quietly.

'She has,' he assured her, adding with cool irony, 'Why do you imagine I was so angry?'

He walked out, and she turned to look at the blank face of the door, her head swimming and her heart pounding. It was probably because of *Abuela* after all, but it did not explain why he had called her Kate. She stifled a small hope, a hope she didn't want at all. There was such a thing as insanity, but it didn't run in her family and she wasn't about to invite it in by thinking in any other way but with annoyance about Diego, because he would never be anything other than what he was now—not to her.

Kate got ready for dinner and then went to face *Abuela*. To her surprise, when she began to apologise she received only a hug as she sat next to the old lady.

'I shall say nothing at all,' Doña Elvira promised. 'You have had a fright, and, as to scolding, I imagine that Diego has already done that.'

'You could say that,' Kate assured her ruefully, her face colouring as her heart leapt at the sound of his name.

'He was greatly concerned,' the old lady chuckled. 'He left here like someone with the devil on his shoulder when he drove to rescue you. The mountains are not always tranquil, child. I will just ask you to remember that.'

Kate nodded. She would remember for the rest of her life, a life she owed to Diego's speed of reaction.

At dinner she was surprised to find Javier home, and he told her that the police had closed the road temporarily. There was another, but longer route apparently, and she wished she had known about that. Nobody, it seemed, was about to enlighten Javier about her exploits, and she dared not look at Diego. He didn't speak to her all evening, but once again the dark eyes captured hers every time she looked up.

CHAPTER EIGHT

IT RAINED for two days, but Kate stayed resolutely at her work. The men arrived late each day, the shorter route being closed still, but they came and the work progressed quickly now. An efficient phone call by Diego had brought the paint, and he was passing when it arrived. His disgusted look spoke volumes. He could have done that in the first place if she had been willing to ask for assistance. His flashing black gaze said it all.

He didn't just irritate her now. She was uneasy with him, hiding from a truth that was well within her grasp if she cared to look for it. The state of the roads did not stop him from going off with his usual regularity, and it was the feeling of loss that his going left her with that drove Kate to accepting Javier's offer of an evening out the next time he asked.

To her surprise, he took her to a casino, the sort of place she had never been to before. It was quite splendid, and she was glad she had a dress of dark blue silk and had dressed up well for the evening.

The building was old, in the heart of the city, and she was unprepared for the sight of the splendid façade and the glitter of the interior. There was a crowded dining-room where the floor at the centre was already packed with dancing couples, but it was the casino itself that drew Javier, his eyes glittering with excitement that was nothing at all to do with Kate's presence.

She could tell as they ate their meal that, although he was obviously enjoying her company, it was the thought

of gambling that was at the very front of his mind. She
was rather startled when he dropped his head and muttered under his breath.

'What's wrong?' Kate felt only amusement. He was
suddenly a bad boy by the look of him, and his grin at
her was rueful.

'Diego has just walked in with Cristina. I did not for
one moment imagine he would be here tonight. I thought
he was going to be out all night, in fact. He does not
fully approve of my hobby.'

'What hobby is that?' Kate asked innocently.

'The tables,' he confessed a little sheepishly. 'I was
about to introduce you to the art, but he will spot us
and intervene.'

'I doubt it,' Kate said wryly. She was sure that Diego
didn't care at all what she did, and she hoped he did not
spot them. She was well aware that she didn't want to
see him with Cristina Serrano.

Her hopes were dashed seconds later, as a waiter murmured his apologies and brought two more chairs to their
table.

'I hope you approve?' Diego said coolly, glancing at
Kate almost as if she were not there at all, and then con-
centrating on his brother. 'It seems a little unfriendly to
occupy two tables when we are part of the same family.'

'No. We—we're glad to see you, are we not, Kate?'
Javier glanced at Kate for support, but she didn't feel
too helpful—not with Cristina hanging on to Diego's
arm and flashing unfriendly looks in her direction.

'Delighted,' she murmured, looking away.

It did nothing at all to put Diego off his decision to
join them, and she had an uncomfortable time
throughout the meal, trying to avoid talking to them. It

was only as Cristina too showed anxiety to be at the tables that Diego stood and asked Kate to dance.

'I thought we were going to the next room...?'

She looked hopefully at Javier, but his passion to be with her was completely lost and Cristina was clearly an unexpected ally.

'Plenty of time, Kate. Dance with Diego and then we'll see.'

'We will indeed,' Diego murmured sardonically as they moved on to the floor, and she turned her head in time to see Javier and Cristina making their way to the casino as if their lives depended on it.

She glanced up at Diego and he looked down at her with mocking black eyes.

'They're gamblers?' she asked in astonishment.

'Only amateurs,' he assured her ironically. 'Surely you know that every Spaniard is a gambler at heart?'

'Are you?'

'I suppose so, in a way. I gamble in business though. Javier finds his excitement at the tables from time to time.'

'And Cristina?'

'She will have other things to do before long, I expect.'

When they got married. He couldn't mean anything else. Kate tried not to stiffen, but she realised she was a very boring companion, and she was not at all surprised when he led her off the floor and made his way to the casino proper, his hand lightly at her elbow.

It was a revelation. The great high ceiling was made of blue glass that shone in the lights. Huge crystal chandeliers hung on golden chains, and the walls seemed to be panelled in silk. She actually came to a halt to stare around and Diego looked down at her in amusement.

'If you are addicted to anything, I can see it is the décor,' he mocked, looking down at her.

'It's a bit over the top,' she murmured, her eyes searching the glittering ceiling that seemed to be soaring our of sight. Her eyes were still on it as he led her forward to where Javier and Cristina stood at the tables.

'Your partner,' Diego said coolly to his brother, and Javier had the grace to look sheepish again.

'I'm sorry, Kate,' he pleaded. 'Sometimes it take ages to get a place, and you can see we haven't succeeded yet.'

'There's plenty of time,' Cristina pointed out. 'It is only ten. I did not rush my meal to be cheated out of playing. Perhaps your English cousin will feel tired, Diego?' she added in a taunting voice.

'She is working all day and not able to lie in bed until noon,' Diego suddenly said sharply. 'Play by all means. I will take Kathryn home.'

Kate was too stunned to be annoyed that he had returned to his formal way of speaking when he said her name, and Cristina was more stunned still.

'Don't you want to play, Kate——?' Javier asked in embarrassment, but Diego cut in yet again.

'She does not,' he answered before she could get out a word. 'One gambler in the family is quite enough. We will leave you to it. In any case, Cristina has her own car so she does not need me at all.'

Cristina went very red at his remark about one member of the family being enough, and she tossed back her head in the way that Kate had noticed in the photograph of her mother.

'If you prefer the company of your cousin to mine...'

'Rarely,' Diego murmured. 'Tonight, though, she seems to have been deserted. She needs me, I think.'

'I can come!' Javier started, moving to leave the tables, but Diego stopped him at once.

'Why, of course not. Stay and enjoy yourself. To-morrow is Sunday and we can all rest.'

Kate was out into the cooler night air before she could really decide what this little play had been about. In the car she turned on him.

'Why did you do that?' she asked angrily. 'You made me look like a spoilt child demanding to be taken home, and you made Javier seem most ungracious, as if he were a boy.'

'You will perhaps realise now the inadvisability of being escorted by my brother,' he pointed out calmly. 'Cristina, too, needed a sharp lesson. As to being a boy, he often acts like one.'

'You certainly don't!' Kate snapped, irritated at being used to dish out lessons to Javier and Cristina.

'You wish me to behave like a hot-headed youth?' he enquired tauntingly. 'What would you do then, Kathryn? Would you look at me loftily and put me in my place? I know my place, it is to be in charge of the *monasterio*, the business of the family and my own state of mind. I am what I am.'

'An irritating, cold-blooded male,' Kate finished sarcastically.

'I find that more acceptable,' he murmured, starting the car and driving off, his eyes cold and staring straight ahead.

It was certainly a longer route to the *monasterio*, and Kate was almost asleep when they finally pulled into the courtyard. The fact that Diego had come the whole way in silence had not made her feel anything but edgy, and drowsiness was the best way to combat it.

'We have arrived,' he said quietly as the car stopped and she opened her eyes.

'So I see.' She moved to get out, but his hand on her arm stopped her.

'Do not encourage my brother,' he said tightly. 'He is no match for you now, and there is a girl who is extremely fond of him. She will make a good wife for Javier and fit in very well here. Both *Abuela* and my mother approve of her.'

'I've no intention of encouraging Javier,' Kate said bitterly, trying to snatch her hand away. 'Does *Abuela* approve of Cristina?'

'Not particularly.' He looked at her intently. 'Nor does my mother, as you no doubt noticed.'

'How awkward for you,' Kate taunted. 'When you marry Cristina there's going to be trouble here.'

Suddenly, her eyes felt hot with tears, and she fought back the reason for it that tried to edge into her mind.

'I am capable of managing trouble,' he jeered softly. 'After all, I manage you, and you are almost as much trouble as Lucia.'

'*Abuela* loved her,' Kate said unhappily, turning away.

'She loves you too,' he said angrily, 'but you will also leave her. It is small wonder, is it not, that I find love to be a shallow emotion?'

'Well, unfortunately there's nothing else but hatred to take its place,' Kate countered.

'There is desire. I cannot believe that someone with your fiery nature has not felt that.'

'You have very odd beliefs,' Kate muttered, her face flushed and anxious in the soft lights from the house.

The midnight-black eyes glanced across at her, the force of his gaze making her tremble.

'Oh, I am not utterly indifferent to you. If I were I would not be so willing to kiss you better when you have worked yourself up to a state of tension. I would not be willing to reach for you when you look desperate. You do sometimes linger in my mind.'

'Thank you! I don't want you to have that trouble, though. Pretty soon the *sala* will be finished and then I'll go back to London. When I have to keep my promise and visit *Abuela* we could perhaps correspond first. You can tell me when you'll be away and I'll plan my visits accordingly, as we obviously can't stand the sight of each other!'

'I do not remember saying that,' he murmured, reaching for her as she tried to open the car door. 'I have told you that I am not entirely indifferent to you. I have also said that there is desire.'

She was in his arms before she could move, his fingers threaded through her hair, his body leaning over her as the cool, perfect lips closed over her own. She fought madly, but he had no trouble at all holding her.

'*Dios!* Be still!' he rasped. 'You have been waiting for this, as I have, all the evening!'

'It's not true!' Kate gasped, trying to turn her face away, horrified that this time he was not generating that peculiar peace but a heady, growing excitement.

'It is true. Why do you imagine you wish to fly at me so frequently? Why do we fight all the time? Your lover is weak, and you, little cousin, need a strong and firm hand.'

'I'm not your cousin!' Kate managed hotly, twisting in his arms. It was a big mistake.

'No, you are not,' he said thickly. 'I am very grateful for that fact.' He caught her closer, and all argument ended as he swooped down to capture her lips and part them masterfully.

She knew she had to fight. It was an instinct of self-preservation. Soon she would go down in a tide of sensation and she would never recover. She wanted to be close to him, crushed against this man who despised her so much that he had engineered her stay here merely to please his grandmother. He had no thought for her at all except contemptuous amusement.

'Kate.'

As his lips lifted momentarily she bit out at him, using the only weapon she had, her breath fast and uneven. It was only the quick flick of his head that saved him from a bite, and he retaliated immediately, his white teeth taking her bottom lip firmly, with just enough pressure to warn her that this line of attack would prove to be very painful. He had said he would be able to deal with her, and he could. Kate had found her match, a man so powerful that she felt molten in his arms.

She froze instantly, waiting for the pain to come, but it never did; instead he released her lip slowly before catching it again with his own lips, his tongue running along the length of it until her tight restraint brought a small whimper of denial from her throat. For a second his eyes flashed to her face before his mouth covered hers again with passionate violence.

She had no idea what was happening. The feeling that seared through her was utterly new, and so unacceptable that she gave a soft, anguished cry. But the need to be free had vanished like magic. Her whole body had relaxed, and she was kissing him back with an almost feverish need.

His hand ran down her back, tracing her spine, helping her to fight herself closer, and she knew it was exactly what she was trying to do. They were in the middle of a whirlwind of sensation, a vibrant awareness in both of them that was all fierce sexual recognition. Everything was spinning. She was crushed to his chest, even that not close enough, and her arms were tightly around his neck.

From some deep inner strength Kate managed to tear her lips away, twisting her head frantically when he came after her at once.

'No!' She forced her hands against his chest, only now conscious that they had been clinging to his neck. 'I don't even like you. We were enemies on sight!'

'Much more than that,' he said harshly, no sign of the elegant and sophisticated man left, only raw masculinity that had been frustrated. His eyes were black pools, and she could see the heavy lashes against them, smell the fresh, sharp fragrance of his skin and the darker flavour of desire. Tiny beads of perspiration stood out on his forehead, and she knew that his hand was moving slowly along the length of her thigh, his fingers flexing tentatively.

'I—I didn't kiss you! It was you who... I have a life of my own!'

'And a lover,' he grated. 'Remember that when Javier turns his attention to you again. He is no match for you at all, and I will not have upheaval in my family ever.'

'I'm going home!' She realised that they were still pressed close together, and pulled away, her heart almost stopping when for a second he refused to release her.

'It would perhaps be wise if you did. For a long time there my uppermost thought was one of great gladness that you were not after all a relative. There was little doubt in my mind as to what was about to happen.'

'You—you can't say that!' Kate looked at him in wild confusion and his glance flared over her.

'I have said it. I am not much given to subterfuge!' He turned away angrily, his hand running over the back of his neck. 'Tomorrow I am going to the Rioja. I will be away for a week. Finish the *sala* and go home. Whenever I know you are to visit *Abuela* I will arrange to be away.'

Kate opened the door, and this time he did not stop her as she almost ran to her room. She had wanted him to come after her, to apologise, to make things better, but she knew he would not. He was right—she must finish the *sala* and go, because Diego was beginning to mean far too much to her, his face constantly in her mind, the wild passion she had felt in his arms utterly new in her life.

He was going to marry Cristina, she was sure. He had almost said so. What did she care? She flung off the beautiful dress and got ready for bed. She couldn't sleep, though. She felt as if she would never sleep again. She paced about her room in her robe, trying to deny the feelings that were taking hold of her. The windows to the courtyard were open, and she stood there for a while trying to draw peace from the still night, but it was a useless task.

Footsteps below her had her looking down, and Diego walked out. As she watched he began to pace about restlessly, his hands deep in his pockets, and she could not tell whether the stiffness of his shoulders was from anger or the same feelings that gripped her too. It was probably anger. Javier had not yet returned, and Cristina was with him.

He suddenly looked up and she drew back quickly, hoping he hadn't seen her. She should have done that at once, as soon as he had come out. She felt the need to move back into the room stealthily, because he was sure to make some wrong and angry judgement as to why she had been standing there.

She sighed and shakily began to get ready, taking off her robe, turning startled as the door opened and Diego stood there, his dark face filled with masculine aggression. He moved further into the room, his hands clenched by his sides as the burning eyes swept over her slender figure in the satin nightdress.

'You were watching for Javier?'

'I was not!' She glared at him in her turn, not at all surprised that he had thought that. After all, she was always wrong, according to him. 'And will you kindly leave?' she added sharply. 'This is my room, not the *sala*.'

'You will not allow my brother to escort you again. I require a promise from you.'

Suddenly Kate's misery left her. Here he was demanding things, treating her as if she were some *femme fatale*, when not long ago he had kissed her and confessed to desire. It was all Diego would ever feel. He was cold all through.

'You'll get no promise at all!' she snapped. 'You may rule this place and everyone in it, but you don't rule me. I'm probably safer with Javier than I am with you. In any case,' she added scathingly, 'when you're in the Rioja I'll do exactly as I like!'

'Then I will cancel my trip.' He moved slowly forward, his step menacing. 'I do not wish to return here to find the place in a turmoil.'

'Don't cancel things on my behalf,' Kate said bitterly, turning away. She made a sort of frantic grab for her robe. 'I'll promise anything just to be rid of you.'

'Will you?' He came behind her and draped the robe around her shoulders, his hands lingering there. 'I am not too easy to dismiss, not for you, Kathryn. In a strange sort of way, you need me, don't you?' he persisted when she kept silent.

'No! I'm more than capable of dealing with anyone.'

'Except me.' Her voice was unsteady and he heard it. 'You have never found another man who was a match for you. You are no longer a girl. If Javier were to make unwelcome advances, you would devastate him with your tongue.'

'Then there's no need to stay. Unless you want to protect him from my wickedness.'

He turned her to face him, his eyes lancing over her. 'Perhaps I only want an excuse to stay,' he suggested softly.

Kate stared up at him, her eyes wide and blue, anger draining away as the dark, dark eyes held hers, and they were like that as Javier passed her door, which was wide open. They had been so wrapped up in each other that they had not heard his step on the stairs, and he paused in the open doorway, his glance moving from one to the other.

'I can see why you relieved me of the responsibility of Kate,' he remarked tightly, before striding off to his own room.

Diego merely raised one dark eyebrow, but Kate was flushed with embarrassment.

'How do you think this looks to him?' she snapped, stepping away from Diego and fastening her robe angrily.

'I imagine he thinks that I am very interested,' he murmured sardonically. 'That being the case, he will watch his step in future. He does not like to get on the wrong side of me.'

So that was what this was all about, a planned accident, just as bringing her home had been planned, and the trip to the coast. Her face went pale and she looked at him bitterly.

'You can improve things further,' she pointed out coldly. 'Tell him about my flat in London and the men in my life!'

For just one second there was murder in the black eyes, and then he spun round and strode from the room, and Kate sank down at the edge of the bed, trembling all over. Whatever she did he would think ill of her. He might as well imagine the worst.

In spite of her unhappiness, Kate slept, and the first rays of the sun were penetrating her room when she found herself being gently shaken into wakefulness.

'Kathryn.'

The sound of Diego's voice had her eyes opening instantly, and she felt a wave of fear to see him crouched by her bed, his dark eyes intently on her as his hand shook her shoulder.

'What is it?' She struggled to sit, perfectly sure that *Abuela* must be ill to have brought him here at this hour.

'Nothing to alarm you,' he assured her. 'Today spring is here and I have something to show you.'

She looked around puzzled, and he laughed softly.

'It is not here. It is outside. Hurry, I want you to look as the sun hits the valley.'

'I'll have to get dressed.'

'No! Come as you are. There is no time.'

He stood and walked to her wardrobe, impatiently pulling open the doors and taking out her thick dressing-gown.

'This will do. You will not be cold.'

He held it out, expecting her to simply get up as she was and walk towards him, and Kate sighed resignedly, throwing back the covers and walking across in her white nightdress. He had seen her like that last night, so what did it matter?

He said nothing. She wasn't even sure if he noticed. There was a burning impatience to get her out of doors to see this thing, whatever it was. She began to fasten her robe, but she was not quick enough for him apparently; his hands moved hers aside, and he finished the task himself before hurrying her out of the room and down the stairs. He could be so annoying, she thought frustratedly. He was also quite impossible to understand. Last night he had practically ordered her home. This morning he was here at dawn to collect her like a lover on a secret tryst. Her face flooded with colour at the thought, and she was glad he was too intent on his expedition to notice.

It wasn't cold out in the courtyard, but it was decidedly chilly. Diego was in dark trousers and a bright sweater, and she grumbled to herself as he hurried her around the side of the house. He hadn't just got out of a warm bed and been dragged into the open air.

'Stop muttering!' he said sternly. 'I promise that it will be worth your efforts.'

At this speed she would soon be warmed up, Kate thought wryly as he kept up the same impetus. He stopped at the low wall at the back of the house, and she looked at him in surprise. As far as she could tell, there was nothing to see at all.

'What——?' she began in an exasperated voice, and he shook his head with equal exasperation.

'Sometimes I know perfectly well why you irritate me,' he said mockingly. 'Look!'

He took her shoulders firmly and turned her to the valley, where the sun was now racing across from the back of the mountains. It was like seeing a stage as the lights came on with one long sweep, and her gasp of wonder was all the sound she made.

As the valley came to life a new and wonderful sight met her eyes. The acres of barren, stunted trees were filled with blossom, each hillside covered with them, more than it was possible to count. The colours were from a fairy-tale, white to palest pinks and lilacs, nothing of the dry-looking wood left, heavy pale blossom as far as the eye could see, a child's picture of fairyland.

'Oh!' Kate's face was filled with delight. There was too much beauty to drink in; her eyes looked and looked, but there was too much to fully penetrate her senses.

'It pleases you, Kathryn?' Diego's deep voice brought her out of a timeless trance, but her eyes would not look away.

'It's beautiful!' she whispered.

'When you were here before you were too late in the season,' he said softly. 'It is a sight too beautiful to miss. Look at the Cristo.'

She looked, another gasp leaving her lips as she saw that the Cristo too had a carpet of pale blossom, the sun just striking the magnificent, awe-inspiring face.

'Oh! Thank you, Diego! Thank you so much!' She turned to him with glowing eyes, and he looked down at her for a second, a smile edging his lips.

'Come,' he said softly. 'We will make the whole thing worthwhile. We will go up to the Cristo.'

'I'm not dressed.' She felt a moment of panic, but he simply ignored it.

'You will be in the car. It will be too cold up there for you to stand outside.'

'But what will people think if they see me come back like this?'

'You were not at all alarmed that I should see you like that; do you fear others more?'

'You made me come,' she said breathlessly as he hurried her along.

'I could not wait for you any longer,' he said determinedly. 'I have been awake for hours.'

She was in the car and he was backing out of the garage before she could protest further, and as he left the courtyard and headed for the winding road at the end of the valley she smiled. What did it matter if the whole of Spain saw her? She was here with Diego and he was not angry at all. She suddenly realised that he could be wonderful.

The road to the Cristo wound round upon itself, a few heart-stopping drops to the side, but Diego drove skilfully and fast, taking them higher and higher until they were driving along the flat road at the base of the mighty statue. It was more breathtaking than ever close up. He stopped the car and she strained to see the whole thing until he laughed softly and opened the door.

'A few seconds only, then,' he said quietly, coming round to help her out.

The wind was chill, but she drew her dressing-gown closely around her and gazed her fill at the mighty figure that towered above them. The blossoms looked no more real at closer quarters and Diego spoke softly.

'Look at the valley. From here you can see it all.'

She turned and could not believe her eyes. For miles and miles the blossom stretched, looking from here like a carpet of beauty. The rain had brought life to the hillsides. Wild flowers had sprung up, brilliantly coloured, taking away the stark grandeur and replacing it with light and gaiety.

The small white church was brilliant in the sunlight, but the lacy blossom was the thing that overwhelmed all, filling the land as far as it was possible to see, a land of pale blossom, beautiful and magical.

'Why—why did you bring me?' she asked tremulously, suddenly aware that Diego was close behind her.

'Perhaps merely to please you,' he said quietly.

She turned her head and looked up at him, and his hand touched hers.

'You are cold. Get back in the car and we will go for breakfast.'

It disappointed her that his smile had died, and she struggled to keep her feelings hidden as she hurriedly got into the car and closed the door. He looked a little grim as he came round and got in beside her, and for a moment he looked across the valley, his face tight.

'I have spent the better part of the night thinking,' he admitted soberly. 'I have imagined you back in England and free of us.' The midnight-black eyes glanced across at her, the force of his gaze making her tremble. 'I have tried to picture the sort of life you lead. Do you enjoy it? Do you go out often, to the theatre, to restaurants?'

'Of course,' Kate managed quietly. 'I don't just sit in my little flat.'

'You are a very modern woman,' he said, almost accusingly. 'There must be men in your life.'

She turned sideways, facing him, her cheeks flushed.

'What are you asking me, Diego? Do you want to know who I sleep with?'

'No!' His voice was savage, none of the quiet companionship left. 'I have thought about that too, and decided that it is none of my business. You are not, after all, my cousin. Your life is your own!'

He started the car and swung it around in the small space, their descent too furious and fast, and almost before she knew it Kate was back at the *monasterio* and in her room. For one moment he had been angry, jealous, and she stood and looked at herself in the long mirror, unable to make any effort to dress for breakfast. All the wonder had gone, but a vibrant yearning had taken its place. He was quite right, she needed him. She wanted him to need her too.

He left, after all. When Kate finally went down to breakfast he was already gone, and she faced the day with none of her usual enthusiasm. Javier was there and his mood was petulant.

'You have seen the blossom,' he remarked nastily. 'I noticed Diego going to your room this morning.'

It was a comment inviting trouble, and Liliana's eyes were startled. She was on the edge of being shocked, as Javier had meant her to be.

'Yes, it's so beautiful. It was kind of Diego to come and wake me. I never saw it when I was here before.' She turned to Liliana with a smile. 'He drove me right up to the Cristo.'

'He probably wanted to see how the church looked with the blossom around it,' Javier cut in caustically before his mother could speak. 'He intends to marry Cristina in that church.'

It was like a sharp knife thrust into Kate, almost catching her off guard. For once in her life she had no ready answer, and Liliana's face was tight with annoyance. She clearly did not approve of Cristina Serrano, but Kate had no doubt whatsoever that Diego had made up his mind with no thought of any approval from his family.

Javier left, his little seeds of destruction cleverly sown, and Kate went to the great *sala* to begin work even before the men arrived. It was quiet, the sunlight streaming in and catching the red and gold of the roof, the deep blues and pastel shades of the frescos. It was almost finished, and then she could go. When she came here again she would contrive not to see Diego, and when he married she would not come at all.

It wasn't just this house and the two women who had reached her heart. She was even fond of Javier, though he behaved like a spoilt child frequently. It was Diego. From wild irritation and annoyance, her feelings had changed. The whole place was empty when he was not there, and it would always be like that. Gradually he had forced his way into her heart as no other person would ever do. Like her mother, she had found the right man, but unlike her mother's man, he had found someone else.

CHAPTER NINE

IT WAS a long week. Javier moved from sulking to trying again to flirt with her, and finally she had to speak to him severely.

'I'm not a girl, Javier,' she said quietly but firmly. 'I'm grown up and not at all manoeuvrable. This sort of thing will only annoy me. I like you better when you treat me as a cousin.'

'And how do you like my brother to treat you?' he asked tightly, his lips once more petulant.

'With Diego I don't have a choice of treatment,' Kate said softly. 'He dislikes me.'

'And you...?'

'Let it go, Javier!' she said sharply, greatly relieved when he did.

It all added to her determination to get things to the state where the great *sala* needed no further attention from her, and, as the week drew to a close, so did the work. Once more she had worked hard, but it was worth it all. The place looked beautiful and she was almost free. She could go any day.

On Saturday morning Liliana was going out for the day, and Javier was obviously preparing to go on some sort of excursion. At any rate he seemed excited, and Kate had no doubt at all that there was some new woman involved, unless he had finally decided to pay some attention to the girl he was being urged to marry.

'Why not come with me, Kathryn?' Liliana invited. 'You have worked harder than ever this week, and the *sala* is almost finished. I will be out all day and *Abuela* is sure to sleep most of the afternoon and evening.'

'I'd rather not, thank you,' Kate smiled. 'I'll sit in the garden and enjoy the rest. I don't mind being alone.'

Liliana was doubtful, but Kate did not want to go with her and spend her time being affable with people she didn't know. She didn't feel affable. She felt downright miserable.

It was only when they had gone and the house was silent that she remembered the furniture in the attics. She had been too involved with other things to get the old furniture restored, and it would keep her here. If she chose the pieces now the men could come to collect them on Monday, and she could leave a plan as to where they were to be placed. Then she could go home and try to forget Diego all over again.

It was silent in the great vaulted roofs of the *monasterio*, but the sunlight still streamed in through the high windows. From up here you could see for miles, and it seemed to be completely cut off from the rest of the house. The original pegged beams still held up the high roof and, apart from her excursion here with Liliana, it seemed as if nobody had ever walked these floors since the house had indeed been a monastery.

She began to move about methodically. When the sun finally moved there would be no light up here, and she wanted everything settled in her mind today. There was plenty to choose from, but only a very few pieces were suitable, although they were veritable treasures.

She became absorbed, and it was only as the light faded that she knew the sunlight had moved to the other side of the *monasterio* and that soon these vaulted rooms would be in near darkness. She had done what she had set out to do, though, and she moved to the great door that would lead her downstairs and into light. It was closed.

At first Kate couldn't believe it, but vaguely she remembered how it had swung so easily when she had come up with Liliana, and how Liliana had chocked it with an old piece of wood. The reason was clear. There was no inside handle. At some time it had dropped off, probably years ago, and a piece of metal had been placed across the gap. She was securely trapped.

She looked at her watch. It was just possible to see it. Four o'clock. Liliana would not be back until very late, and as to Javier, if he went to the casino he would do very well to be in by midnight. *Abuela* would be asleep, with Ester drowsing in her chair by the bed, and, in any case, it was three storeys down in this solid stone house. Her only chance was that a servant would be upstairs and would hear her. She began to bang on the door, shouting as loudly as she could.

It must be at least six o'clock. Kate could no longer see her watch in a room that was now almost completely dark. Her hands were numb with banging, her throat hoarse, and she sank to the floor by the side of the door wondering if anyone would ever find her up here. It was not as silly as it sounded. The only silly thing was herself coming up here and telling no one where she was.

She climbed on a table yet again to see from the window, but the drop was terrifying with few hand-grips and she would only get out of there as a last resort—tomorrow. The thought of spending the night here was really frightening and it renewed her energy. She began to bang and shout again.

She had sunk back to the floor when the door opened, and she looked up to see Diego standing there. It was too dark in the room to see him clearly, but behind him were the lights on the twisting stone stairs and she jumped up, rushing towards him, shaking with relief when his arms came around her and he held her close.

'I was locked in! I couldn't get out! I've been here for hours! Oh, Diego, please hold me!'

She tightened her arms around his neck and he drew her out into the light, closing the door behind them. His eyes flared over her, lingering on the white face that was streaked with dust, and he swept her up into his arms, making his way back down the stone stairs.

'How do you survive?' he muttered. 'I should lock you in your room and feed you through a trapdoor, but even then you would fall in the shower and bang your head.'

'The door swung shut,' she said urgently, her voice little more than a whisper now after all the shouting. 'It was too high to get out of the window.'

'Madre de Dios!' His arms tightened, and she suddenly felt so exhausted that she put her head against his shoulder and closed her eyes. Maybe he wouldn't tell her off until later? She couldn't seem to think of anything at all, except that he was back and she felt safer than she had done in her whole life.

He took her to her room and sat her in a chair, looking at her severely.

'You will stay exactly there,' he ordered. 'I will get you a hot drink and something strong to go with it. Do not move one inch until I return.' He shook his head in exasperation, walking out and leaving her feeling shaken and bemused. How was it that he was always there when she needed him? Even when she was a girl of seventeen he had been on hand to rescue her from Javier's attempts at seduction.

She went to get a shower. She felt dirty and bruised after her long time in the attics and her hammering at the door, and her knee was painful where she had banged it in climbing down from looking out of the window. The hot water was blissful.

Diego was back sooner than she had expected.

'Kathryn!'

As soon as he saw she was missing he roared for her, and she hurried stumbling from the shower before she angered him further. She tried to shout to him, but her voice seemed to have gone completely, and she only just had time to wrap a large towel around her before he was there, standing in the bathroom doorway to glare at her.

'You are the most disobedient, wilful woman in the world!' he roared. 'Why did you not reply?'

She shook her head and stared at him fearfully, clutching the white towel around her, her toes curling anxiously into the cream carpet on the floor.

'I...I...'

It was all she could get out, and realisation dawned on him quickly, his anger dying to be replaced by one of his amused and brilliant smiles.

'So, firebird! You have lost your great weapon. The tongue is silent.'

He strode across and stopped the shower, urging her into the bedroom and collecting her thick robe as if he had every right in the world. He held it out for her, and she managed to get herself into it without too much embarrassment, well aware all the time that he was laughing softly at her predicament. When it was fastened around her he turned her to look at him, his dark eyes glittering with amusement.

'I really think that you are at my mercy,' he mused softly. 'I will think about it. Meanwhile, drink your tea and sip this brandy. I will go away to consider how to take advantage of this situation.' He turned at the door, his glance flaring over her. 'You will remain here, safely in your room. If I find you wandering about I will take great pleasure in spanking you. You may appear for dinner. In the meantime, rest. I think that, even for a girl who is as good as the next man, you have had quite a fright. I believe they used to lock recalcitrant monks up there and forget all about them,' he added, his eyes flashing with amusement when all she could do was stare at him.

She couldn't seem to look away, and slowly the laughter died from his eyes.

'The more I see of you, the more I become sure that you need me,' he said softly. 'Perhaps if you had a voice you would admit it.'

Not for anything in the world. There was Cristina, and he would never love anyone. He would never feel as she felt. Kate lowered her head. She had no voice to fight him off, but she could look away. He left quietly and, contrarily, she wished he had stayed.

She fell asleep, only waking in time for dinner, and although her voice was a little hoarse it had come back to a certain extent. Javier was nowhere to be seen, but Liliana was back, and as Kate came into the smaller *sala* Diego turned and looked at her intently. She was amazed to realise after a minute that he had said nothing at all to his mother about her afternoon adventure. She had to confess herself when Liliana enquired about her husky voice.

'I locked myself in the attics,' she said, shamefaced, aware of Diego's eyes on her. 'I shouted for hours and then . . . then Diego came home and found me.'

'Oh, Kathryn! It is my fault. I should have impressed on you that the door needs to be kept open. I was locked in there myself when I was first married. I was terrified. Gerardo was most amused,' she added with a reminiscent smile.

Like father, like son. Diego sat back and just looked at her, and Kate's face began to burn.

'It was my own fault,' she said quickly. 'I was rushing around getting things done, as usual.'

'It is not really funny, though,' Liliana continued, having listened in surprise to Kate's new husky voice. 'You might have been there all night.'

'She was contemplating the windows,' Diego offered quietly, and Liliana looked quite shaken.

'Kathryn! I did not contemplate that for one moment when I was trapped up there. You have a bolder nature than I.'

'And is likely to live for less time,' Diego put in sardonically. 'While she is here we should hire a keeper.'

'I've nearly finished,' Kate informed him huskily. 'Next week I can go back to London and the office.'

He just looked at her steadily, the dark eyes enigmatic, and Liliana looked sad.

'Oh, Kathryn,' she said quietly. 'I shall miss you so much. You have become part of our lives.'

Kate waited for Diego to add that she had become part of *Abuela's* life too, but he said nothing at all. Instead the dark eyes seemed to burn her all through the meal, and she was glad to escape to her room after coffee.

She didn't make it to her room. As she left Diego followed, and once again she felt the strong hand on her arm. He said nothing at all, but turned her in the direction of his study, and such was his hold over her by now that she simply went with him with no question whatsoever. She had a fair idea of what he was about to say.

'When do you intend to leave?'

He closed the door and leaned against it, his face still. There was nothing in his expression to give her any clue as to his feelings.

'Early next week. Perhaps Wednesday. If the men can collect the furniture on Monday I can leave a plan where everything has to go.'

'Do you usually do this? I would have thought that a person who worked for perfection would have stayed to see any project completed.'

'Normally,' she confessed huskily, 'I wouldn't go until everything was done. Normally, though, I don't live where I work. I call at the office each day and go home at night. This time things are slightly different.'

'This time you are with your family and Merrol is miles away,' he said harshly. 'You miss the nightlife too, I expect.'

'As you've made your mind up, I won't argue with you,' Kate said wearily. 'Do you mind if I go to bed? This has not been one of my better days.'

She moved towards him, determined to get out of the room, but he stepped forward and gripped her shoulders tightly, looking down at her furiously.

'You will never come again, I know it! You are deserting this place as——'

'As my mother did—I know!' Kate said bitterly, her throat hoarse. 'Every thing I do, everything I say, you blame me...'

Suddenly he was still, looking at her deeply.

'Do I? Do I blame you so very much? Surely I am there when you need me, my arms ready to hold you? In spite of your belief in my savagery, you turn to me.' His knuckles ran down her cheek, lingering against the rosy flush, and then he lashed his arms around her, his face no longer musing.

'You have promised to return.'

'And I will,' she managed unevenly, struggling to be free of arms that held no love. 'You made a promise too. You said you would always be away when you knew I was coming.'

He let her go, his face still and empty.

'And you want that? You never wish to see me again?'

For a minute she didn't speak, wanting to tell him that she longed to see him every second. What was the use?

'No! You don't care who you hurt just so long as you have tight control. If you want *Abuela* to see me, then just remember it will only be if you're not here. If you are here I'll go straight back home.'

He turned away and she went unsteadily to the door.

'I will not be here,' he assured her in a flat, cold voice.

In her room, Kate let the emotions she had held so tightly in check take over, tears pouring down her face as she undressed. The thought of never seeing Diego again was like a nightmare, a death sentence. She lay on her bed and wept until her eyes ached, and she didn't see the door open, nor did she see Diego watching her.

'So many tears will put out your fire,' he said quietly.

Kate sat up quickly, trying to wipe away the hot tears.

'You think you can just walk in here...' she sobbed bitterly.

'Yes, I think I can just walk in here,' he answered softly, closing the door and walking over to lift her to her feet. 'And I think that you need me as I need you.'

'You don't need anyone. You don't need me especially——' she began, but his arms closed around her tightly, stilling her struggles.

'Do I not?' he asked deeply. 'This is a game we play, a game to cover feelings. I want you as I have never wanted any other woman, and no other man will ever be able to tame such a firebird as you, Kate.'

'Do you want me to be tame?' She looked up at him, her face unhappy with tears, and he wiped them away, his fingers gentle against her cheeks.

'No. I want you as you are, as the woman you promised to be when you were merely a girl. I have resolutely gone away each day, trying to keep away from you when I longed to take you with me.'

'I—I'll come back——'

'No! It will not do any more!' He looked down at her fiercely, his arms tightening. 'I want you here, with me!'

'Until you marry Cristina,' Kate reminded him bitterly.

'Who is Cristina?' he asked softly as his lips closed over hers.

A great surge of joy swept through Kate, and, as his hands cradled her face, her own fingers threaded into the thick, dark hair and rejoiced in the feel of him. He urged her close, and her lips parted obediently as he deepened the kiss until she seemed to be spinning away from the earth.

'You are not tense, *querida*,' he murmured against her skin, 'but you can be as breathless as you like. Whatever happens to you, whatever you feel, I am here.'

Whatever she felt? He had built a dazzling world around her, and she felt nothing but light and magic, her body floating on a cloud as he lifted her.

'Diego.' It was not fear and not a protest, just the desire to hear his voice.

'You are safe with me, Kate,' he assured her gently, as he placed her on the soft bed and came to take her back into his arms. 'There are many ways of loving.'

One long-fingered brown hand touched her cheek. She could feel the warmth of his breath against her face, the warmth of his body close to hers, and her eyes closed languorously as his lips trailed over her skin.

'You told me that you were not a particularly fearful person,' he reminded her softly. 'Are you afraid now?'

She shook her head, her heart beating so wildly that she felt sure he would hear it. He covered it with his hand, his fingers brushing the rise of her breast.

'Look at me then, Kate,' he commanded deeply.

She opened deep blue eyes that were instantly held by the black of his gaze. Again it was almost hypnotic, and she could neither look away nor close the eyes that clung to his. His hand covered her breast as he watched her, and her heart took off on a mad dance of its own that threatened to shake her whole body.

His fingers gently aroused the tight nipple, and his head lowered slowly until his lips covered her own. It was no kiss to drain away her tension this time. As their lips met fire exploded between them, and she was sure it had taken Diego as much off guard as it had taken her, because his hand tightened on the tender swell of her breast and then slid beneath her to lift her close.

Feeling flashed between them, electric and heated, and she gave a small sound of shock as he moved against her convulsively. Their mouths fused and clung as he held her fiercely for timeless minutes, and then he lifted his head, looking into her dazed eyes.

'*Dios!* I said I wanted you. I did not know how much.'

Kate's lips reached for his without even knowing it, her body delighting when his own lips possessively took over, his hands moulding her slender frame. She moved towards him and his body accepted her as if they were each part of the same whole.

'Are you fighting again to be close to me, *querida*?' he asked, his breathing heavy. 'There is no need to fight. I am waiting for you. I have been waiting for you since you came here.' He groaned and crushed her to him. 'I promised you safety. Now I am not so sure of my ability to keep that promise.'

In their frenzied delight with each other, her night-dress had moved from her shoulder, and his teeth bit gently into the satin skin, his lips then caressing the rise of her breast.

'Let me look at you, Kate,' he begged huskily.

He waited for no answer, knowing he needed none. She was pliant and smouldering in his arms, clinging to him, and he slid the nightdress away until the silken beauty of her breasts was unveiled. She gave herself up with a gasp of joy as his lips claimed the tender nub, and then she was twisting against him and beneath him as all caution left Diego and his promise of safety was forgotten.

She wanted to touch him, and her fingers tried to part the buttons of his shirt until he tore them open himself and shrugged out of it, casting it to the floor with his dinner-jacket, his mouth never leaving hers. And then she felt the delight of his skin on her own, the satin dark of his chest against the pale of her breasts, the tingle of dark hair against her more tender skin.

He looked down, seeing her lighter skin against his own, his bronzed chest crushing her.

'Release me from my promise, Kate,' he asked huskily, his eyes flaring with triumph as she shivered against him, her body completely taken over by feeling. 'Say yes to me.'

'Yes.'

It was only a soft gasp, but it was enough. With one strong sweep of his hand he removed the nightdress, his eyes devouring her before he buried his face between her breasts.

'Kate! For so long...'

He covered her with kisses until she was sobbing in his arms, waiting for the fierce possession that would join her to him, and at first she was utterly oblivious to the sound of someone knocking at the door of her room.

'Kate! Kate!'

It was Javier's voice and she moved, raising her head unsteadily.

'No, Kate! Stay with me!' Diego groaned.

'Kate, it's a call from England. Señor Merrol is on the phone.'

Diego raised his head and looked at her, a sensuous flush across his high cheekbones, his eyes glittering. 'Do you go when Merrol calls or stay with me?' he asked hoarsely.

'I—I've got to answer. It's the telephone.'

'Answer, then.' He moved from her and got to his feet, tossing her the robe that lay on the floor by his jacket. For a second his eyes flashed to her, and then he turned away angrily.

'It is almost eleven, ten o'clock in England. Does he sit up all night wondering what you are doing, or is he in some nightclub wishing you were there?'

She refused to answer the angry voice, and slid into her things as he turned his back and put on his shirt. He was still fastening the buttons he had torn open so readily when she went quietly from the room.

Javier was waiting a little way down the passage, and she knew she looked flustered—that was an understatement. She was still shaking all over, a burning ache inside that would not stop.

'I was just coming back to try again,' Javier said quietly. 'I wondered if you had heard me.'

'I—I was asleep,' Kate lied quickly. 'I had to get my—my robe on.'

'I think you were dreaming,' he suggested mockingly, the edge of sarcasm in his voice. 'I thought you were talking to yourself—in two voices.'

'Even if I had been, I doubt if you could have heard through these thick doors,' Kate countered shakily. He looked back to her room and she took his arm in sudden desperation. 'Will you go down with me? I'm still half asleep. I might fall down the stairs.'

He obliged, but she had the feeling that his ears were only attuned to the sound of any movement on the passage. She hurried him along, murmuring about the cost of calls from England, but he was stiff with petulance, hardly listening to her at all.

And it was all for nothing. Felix had just had the urge to ring her, as he said infuriatingly.

'How's it going, Kate?' he asked, when she had finished tearing into him almost tearfully.

'It's finished, all except the final touches. I'll let you know.'

'Photograph it carefully,' he urged seriously, 'and guard the negatives with your life. The best we'll have enlarged and printed. I really think we've got Spain at last!'

She had never felt more like killing him in her life. As she replaced the receiver, though, a small flicker of sanity tried to surface. What was wrong with her? There was Cristina. Diego just wanted her. But she wanted him too, and she loved him; she was enough of a Spaniard to fight for the one man who could make her happy.

He was waiting in the hall as she came from the small *sala* where she had taken the call, and his face was now pale as she walked slowly towards him.

'You are leaving?' He caught her chin in his hand, tilting her face, his other hand hard on her shoulder, and she made a decision she would have to live with.

'No, not if you want me to stay.'

He stared at her, unbelieving, and then crushed her to him, his body shuddering as she came willingly.

'I want you to stay. Have I not been saying it since you came here?' His lips covered hers in a long, deep kiss and then he let her go, his smile rueful. 'It is perhaps as well that he called. I have never before begged to be released from a promise.' His fingers stroked down her soft cheek. 'Tomorrow we will talk, Kate,' he said softly. 'My flare of anger at Merrol has brought me back to my senses.'

She wondered what he meant by that, but she had no time to ponder for long as he held her close and kissed her again before going along the hall to his study. As she climbed the stairs she saw Javier, his face furious and white as he walked away from the head of the stairs, his suspicions confirmed.

In the morning she came down to meet Diego walking angrily from his study, and he took her arm, this time not in his usual demanding grip.

'I have to go out. I wanted to be with you, but there is some sort of trouble at a hotel we are building on the south coast. Come with me.'

'I—I can't. The men——'

'Always it is the men, the *sala*, your work,' he murmured, only partly teasing. 'It is perhaps as well. We would have to stay the night, and who knows what would happen when I had you to myself? Come to the car with me, then.'

His arm came round her shoulder and she snuggled against him willingly, bringing a smile to his rather annoyed face.

'Kate.' He leaned against the car and looked at her, holding her close, tilting her face to the morning sunlight, his eyes skimming the fiery shine of her hair. He bent quickly and kissed her. 'This is merely prolonging the agony. I will be back some time tomorrow, and we will then talk. Meanwhile,' he added sternly, but she didn't let him finish; instead she smiled up into his face.

'No climbing ladders, no visits to the attics, and don't drive a car.'

She received that flashing smile, and then he looked at her oddly. 'I have no wish to trap you. You are a firebird, and would burn yourself to dust.' His hand stroked her glorious hair. 'Wait for me?' he asked almost humbly.

She had never been so happy. The only promise she broke was to take the men up to the attics when they came and point out the furniture she wanted repairing. The piece of wood was her first task, though, and she was amused and quite touched when she found Liliana hovering about anxiously to see that history did not repeat itself.

Then she looked at the great *sala*, her mind placing the furniture, visualising how it would look. It was beautiful, magnificent, and she sighed with satisfaction and went to find her grandmother.

Doña Elvira was very obviously moody, and greeted Kate without her usual joy.

'Liliana has been in to see me earlier,' she said glumly. 'She tells me that the great *sala* is finished.'

'It is. It needs only the furniture, and the older pieces when they're restored. You must come and see it,' Kate exhorted, trying to dispel the gloom on the old face.

'I am not at all sure that I want to. You will be getting ready to leave.' It was on the tip of Kate's tongue to tell her that she was staying, but sheer instinct warned her not to. What had Diego said, after all? What had he promised? Nothing. She was the one deeply in love. Diego had said quite clearly a long time ago that it was only a matter of imagination. He had not even said how long he wanted her to stay. She didn't want *Abuela* to be hurt all over again. When Diego came back they would talk—he had said so. Then was the time to tell *Abuela*.

'I'll be back very often,' she murmured, her face flushed, but the old lady didn't notice.

'I am a selfish old woman.' She patted Kate's hand. 'Run along to the *sala* while I dress. I will come and see the kind of thing that my *nieta* is capable of. According to Liliana and Diego, the *sala grande* now makes the rest of the place look shabby. Perhaps we can keep you busy almost endlessly with one room after the other?' she laughed.

Like the Forth Bridge. Felix *would* be pleased. He would be wanting to turning the *monasterio* into a permanent show-place. She could imagine how Diego would react to that.

The men came and removed all the scaffolding, lingering awe-struck to admire their own work, looking at Kate with the same kind of awe. She had coaxed work from them that they had not known they were capable of, and they parted from her with smiles that were close to affection.

'It is beautiful, *señorita*,' the man who had done the frescos said softly, standing by Kate and looking up at the glory of the high roof.

Yes, it was beautiful. It was transformed, as she was, and the look on her face was softer than it had ever been. Diego had removed the bitterness from her fire and turned it to love. She could never live without him again.

CHAPTER TEN

AFTER dinner Kate went to her room. She was happy. Nothing was certain, but she felt a great satisfaction about her work, and waited with tremulous joy for Diego to come the next day. Her heart leapt foolishly as a soft knock on her door made her imagine that he was already back, although she knew it was impossible. It was Javier.

'I've just been to see the *sala*,' he said as she looked at him in surprise. 'It's very beautiful, Kate. You are something of a genius.'

'Not really. Just well trained and deeply interested,' she assured him, relieved that it was something innocuous and not some new scheme to upset her.

'You are now going home?' he asked quietly, and all her senses became alert. For one moment she had forgotten seeing him at the head of the stairs as Diego had kissed her goodnight, but now she remembered very clearly indeed.

'Perhaps.'

He looked at her seriously for a minute, and then sighed deeply.

'Since last night I have been turning over in my mind what to say—how to let you know——'

'How about telling me straight out—whatever it is?' Kate asked firmly. His expression, saddened and anxious, was beginning to worry her, and, although she could think of nothing whatsoever he could say to alarm her, she was nevertheless beginning to feel the rise of alarm with every second.

'It is Diego,' he began in a rush, going on before her annoyed expression could turn into sharp words. 'He is doing with you exactly what he has done before with so many women, and you know I am fond of you, Kate.'

'I'm sure you are,' Kate said drily, ready to really put him in his place finally, not wanting to hear one single word against Diego.

'It is because of me,' he went on miserably.

'Perhaps you could be a little more explicit?' Kate asked sharply.

'If you like.' He stiffened when it became apparent that she was not going to listen wide-eyed and believe every word he said. 'I have seen you with him, I saw you last night. It is difficult to believe that someone as clever as you, someone who has good reason to remember how he sent you away long ago, should fall under his spell. Everyone I have ever been interested in has received the same fate. Diego takes them from me because he decided long ago whom I would be allowed to marry.'

'I don't believe you!' Kate said angrily.

'I did not expect that you would, but you were sent away very rapidly when you were here before, even though *Abuela* wanted you both to stay. Cristina too was my girl first, and now Diego is going to marry her, which is a fairly final step.'

'Are you telling me that he loves Cristina?' Kate asked quietly, suddenly remembering how he had greeted Cristina Serrano when she had been here, the things he had said later.

'I do not imagine so,' Javier said flatly. 'I doubt if he loves anyone at all, other than *Madrecita* and *Abuela*. He must marry, though, and Cristina is suitable. She is of a good family. They will be married and the reception will be in the *sala grande*. It was always used for such things in the past. That is one of the reasons he was so anxious to have it done.'

It wasn't. It was to keep her here for *Abuela*. But why did he go to such lengths when he had sent her away when she was seventeen, knowing her mother would have to go too? Surely *Abuela* wanted her mother most of all?

'I am only trying to save you pain, Kate,' Javier said stiffly as she stared at him as though he were not there. 'Plenty of women have fallen in love with Diego. He is handsome, rich...he has everything.'

There was a plaintive jealousy, and she heard it, but the seeds of doubt were sown, and as he left she went down to say goodnight to her grandmother, questions tumbling through her mind. And it was wickedly easy to get information from the old lady.

'Always in the past the *sala grande* has been used for important receptions,' she confirmed when Kate asked her what the beautiful room would be used for. 'When I was married, the great reception was held there, although for Liliana it was held at her home. Diego too will hold his reception there, now that the *sala* has been refurbished.'

'Are you sure he will want to?' Kate asked tremulously, hope beginning to die away.

'Why, yes, Kathryn. He has told me,' the old lady said with a long look at her. Was *Abuela* warning her too? She would never say anything against Diego. Liliana had said she loved him, perhaps too much.

'*Abuela?*' Kate turned as she stood at the door, ready to leave her grandmother to settle down for the night. 'I don't want to distress you, but why did you let my mother go so easily when she came back, when I was seventeen?'

Sadness clouded the old face, and Kate regretted the question instantly. It was too late to take it back, though; the damage had been done.

'Diego wished it,' she said quietly. 'He does nothing but for good reason, child. At the time I was happy with his reason, but I did not know that Lucia would die, I was content to wait.' She sighed. 'Now perhaps I am not so patient. One cannot make dreams come true. Things happen, or they do not.'

He had told her that Javier was involving himself with his adopted cousin, a girl of seventeen. She would have been happy to agree when he sent them away, not even imagining that she would outlive the daughter she loved. It seemed only too true.

Javier was in the hall as Kate came back, his face flushed with angry colour.

'You have been to ask *Abuela*,' he accused. 'I should have known that my word would not do for you—that I wished to protect you...'

Coming from Javier, that was very rich indeed, but Kate was not feeling amused; she felt cold deep inside.

'I can protect myself, Javier,' she said quietly. 'I told you I was no longer a girl. I need no protection whatsoever. What I do need is a ride to the airport very early tomorrow. Will you take me?'

For a moment his face paled, and he looked as if he was about to say something else, but Kate had finished talking. She had nothing more to say. She turned to the stairs without waiting for an answer, seeking the quiet of her room, and she was almost halfway up when he came to his senses, his voice following her.

'I'll take you, Kate—if you really want to go.'

'I want to go,' Kate said in a brittle voice, looking down at him. 'Isn't that what you expected, *cousin*?'

His new pallor disappeared in a red flush of embarrassment, and from the look in his eyes she knew that if she had been staying she would have had no further trouble from Javier. In future he would behave himself without any need to ask. Petulant wheedling would get him nowhere with her, and he now knew it. It was a pity, because, in spite of everything, she had a soft spot him.

When she arrived back in London, Kate had to admit that she would never be the same again. The burning drive that had sustained her all her life seemed to have gone as if it had never existed. There was no fire in her now. She had left Spain and the *monasterio*. She had left Diego without waiting to accuse him, but he owned her as if he still held a tight rein that controlled her heart. And what would she accuse him of? He had promised nothing, had offered only desire.

The only good thing was Felix and his kindness. He had met her at the airport, taken one look at her and dealt with everything. He had asked no questions either. She wanted to weep, but not on any other shoulder but Diego's. Dear, safe Felix was no refuge. There was no refuge at all except time.

Her flat seemed dull, dismal after the glory of the *monasterio*, every thought bringing Diego back with a rush, and she was happy indeed to see Felix when he came round in the early evening with a great sheaf of photographs and drawings for a big country house outside London he wanted her to tackle next. She settled to look at them with him thankfully. It would be night soon enough, and then there would be nothing to keep Diego out of her mind.

She was making them a coffee when somebody began to hammer on the door as if they intended to knock it down, and Felix jumped up to answer it before she could get out of the kitchen, his face as startled as hers when he met her in the restricted space of the hall.

'I'll get it,' he joked wildly. 'It's got to be the police with a knock like that. They've caught you at last—hide behind the door.'

He looked a bit anxious, though, and she felt pretty much the same herself. The sound was nothing less than violent, and she was right behind him when he wrenched the door open courageously.

Courage was needed. Diego stood there with the same demonic expression on his face she remembered so well, and his furious look only deepened when he saw Felix.

'You live here?' he asked violently, ignoring Kate.

'No! Of course I—no, I——'

'Then perhaps you would leave?' Diego suggested savagely.

'Well I . . . yes if you like . . . I'll just . . .'

Felix backed off towards the sitting-room as Diego stepped inside, and Kate's eyes began to blaze too as she came out of a sort of stunned trance.

'You'll stay here, Felix!' she snapped, glaring up at Diego and meeting furious looks. 'There's no reason at all for you to leave!'

Felix, though, was busy collecting the plans and photographs together. 'Oh, yes, there is, love,' he muttered, glancing anxiously at Diego's savage face. 'Honestly, there is. I'll see you at work tomorrow.'

He managed to slide past Diego, but he could not escape the voice.

'You will not see her at all! She is going home!'

'Er—right,' Felix got out with breathless treachery, looking extremely relieved as he got to his car.

Diego slammed the door and turned on Kate as she turned on him. He got his words out first.

'I have said that I did not want to know,' he grated, 'but I do. I must know even if it kills me!'

She was too stunned to reply, not understanding for a second, and he grasped her shoulders, giving her a shake, the dark eyes blazing.

'Tell me!' he rasped. 'Is it Merrol? Or does he merely wish to take the place of someone else? Who is it?'

'It isn't anyone,' Kate flared, understanding him at last, still stunned that he was here, and infuriated by his autocratic behaviour. 'I go out with people, sometimes men, but they're only casual friends. They leave me at my door, and even if they didn't it's no business——'

'Always?' he demanded violently, his hands moving to cup her face painfully.

'Always! I never...I've never...but if you imagine you can come here and...'

He took a deep breath that almost seemed to hurt, and she saw with a sort of frightened astonishment that his lips were white, his face tight with the effort of controlling his feelings. The tight grip relaxed a little and his eyes burned into hers.

'If you had said there was someone, some man——!' He stared at her almost violently, and then pulled her into his arms, crushing her against him, frustration in every line of his body, in every strained muscle, his breathing heavy.

'I have spent my nights in an agony of jealousy since you came back to Spain. I will not do so again.'

Kate struggled free. It was now or never, she knew, because if he kept on holding her she would just give in. She turned away, not too surprised when he let her go.

'I don't know what makes you imagine you can come storming in here,' she began tightly, her face carefully turned from him. 'And how did you know that I would have come straight here anyway?'

'I knew you would come straight to your own little hole to burn yourself out. I followed immediately before you could come to any harm. It is my function, is it not?'

'I'm not coming back, so I don't know why you bothered to come,' Kate said unsteadily.

'I came because my brother is too filled with guilt to keep quiet,' he said softly. 'I know what he said to you. He confessed all when he saw my face as I came home and found you gone. I will deal with him later.'

'Not for me,' Kate said bitterly. 'I've finished the great *sala*. You can get married there in style, and don't blame Javier for that bit of information, *Abuela* told me.'

'I am not surprised,' he murmured arrogantly. 'I usually mention my plans to her. The *sala* is incredibly beautiful. You should be proud of it.'

'I am!' Kate snapped. 'I'll be able to imagine you getting married there.'

'I intend to marry at the small, white church,' he informed her cruelly. 'The reception will be held in the *sala grande*. It will be filled with white flowers to offset the red and gold. I have thought it all out.'

'Brilliant. Another genius in the family!'

Kate spun away to walk out and leave him, but he grabbed her, lifting her up and cradling her struggling body against his superb strength.

'You are snapping sparks and flames,' he murmured, holding her still. 'You are burning yourself away. Burn me too, firebird. Come home to Spain and marry me. I have imagined you beside me in the great *sala*, the white of your dress against the gold, the sunlight touching your fiery hair. I will never let the dream go.'

She looked up at him, her eyes wide, her lips parted, and he smiled that brilliant smile that turned her heart over.

'Say yes, my wild and wonderful Kate,' he pleaded softly. 'How will I live if you do not? I love you.'

'Oh, Diego, yes!' Kate cried, winding her arms tightly around his neck. 'How would I live either? I love you too, so much!'

'I am not unaware of it,' he whispered arrogantly as his lips moved hotly on her cheeks.

'You're the most haughty, arrogant, high-handed man in the world,' Kate grumbled, shivering as his lips searched her neck, her ears and her lips.

'But you already know that, *querida*,' he murmured, laughter in his voice. 'You have told me this already.' His laughter died as his eyes met hers. 'I am also the man who loves you like a mad fool, who worries when you are out of his sight, who wants you endlessly.' He slid her to the floor, shuddering when her arms refused to move from his neck, moulding her against him as their lips fused and brought the fire racing between them, until they were once again wild in each other's arms. 'If I do not have you now, I will die of it,' he groaned against her lips. 'You said that there is no man. Tell me that there is me and let me love you. Say yes, *querida*!'

'Yes,' she whispered, her whole body trembling with delight as he lifted her again and moved with her to the bedroom, laying her down on the bed, and looking at her in the soft light of the lamps.

'I am hungry for you, my Kate. But I will wait,' he said softly.

Her arms reached out for him, and he came to her with a low moan of joy, his body covering hers, his desire for her sending thrills over her heated skin. And she was once again wild and restless in his arms, her breathing

fast and uneven as he undressed her, her gasp of pleasure
an echo of his as at last they clung together, his bronzed
skin against the creamy sheen of her own.

'You are everything I have desired, everything I have
waited for for so long,' he murmured against her soft
cheek. 'I have looked at the pale blossom and imagined
that one day you would be there to walk beside me
through the wonder of it, sharing my joy. And you are
more than I dreamed of, more than I hoped for. Tell me
again, Kate, that you love me, that I do not imagine this
heaven.'

'I love you,' Kate whispered, her lips eagerly searching
for his. 'You're peace and safety, gladness and excitement. Oh, Diego, my love!'

Their kisses deepened and deepened until she murmured distractedly and pulled her arms free, her fingers
clenching in the shining jet of his hair. His lips found
her ear, his teeth nibbling at the tender lobe until shivers
of pleasure drove her to search for his mouth with a
growing urgency that was impossible to control.

'This is what you want, *pequeña*? This, and this?' His
mouth opened, his tongue probing into the warmth of
her own, roughly caressing as he ran warm hands over
her, and she surrendered completely, permitting the in-
vasion, her body arching towards him with a desperate
ache that grew by the second.

He seemed to be enveloping her in warmth, his arms
pulling her closer and closer, and she lost herself in the
magic, her limbs liquid, her body completely pliant, a
soft instrument for the skill of his hands.

It was only when she heard her own voice murmuring
his name over and over against his mouth that Kate
became aware that Diego was no longer controlled
himself. His breathing was unsteady, his body as restless
as her own. The firm, sure hands moved with impatient

need over her, his fingers urgently seeking the tender, swollen centre of her breast.

His lips moved slowly and carefully over her face, his breath warm and arousing on her skin, and fierce pleasure surged through her as he rubbed his cheek against the silken tenderness of hers, his hands tightening at her gasp of pleasure.

'What do you want?' he asked unevenly, his lips open over hers. 'You want me to tame you, to take you now and never release you? Shall I tell you what I want? I want your skin against mine like this, nothing between us forever. I want to capture that wild, bright, beauty and take it for myself. I want to make love to you until you beg and fight to get closer!'

She was in an aching torment of need, her hand behind his dark head, trying to force his lips to fuse with her own, but his head swooped down, his teeth sharply painful before his mouth warmly captured her, tugging at the delicate erect nipple until she cried out.

Kate arched wantonly against him, her fingers restless in his hair as his lips left her breast and roamed erotically over the silken curve of her waist and stomach.

'Now?' he murmured thickly. 'Do you want me now, *querida*?'

He held her fast, his eyes burning into hers as he cupped her face, and her fingers sought the smooth, harsh satin of his cheeks, her own cheeks.

'Oh, please, Diego,' she moaned.

He took her with fierce tenderness, his lips covering her frenzied cry until she melted back towards him, and then the midnight-black eyes were burning into hers as he lifted his head.

'My wild, beautiful, Kate,' he whispered hoarsely. 'You belong to me at last. The pain is over, *dulce amor*, and heaven begins.'

It was a heaven she wept to remain in as at last they spiralled back to earth, but strong brown arms enveloped her, and this time her tears were happy. He gently lifted her head from his shoulder when the storm of gladness was past, his eyes warm and adoring.

'Oh, *mi amor*,' he said softly. 'With you life is bright and wonderful, dazzling and filled with joy.' His lean fingers wiped her tears as he smiled at her. 'Did you really think that you could escape from me?'

'I thought there was Cristina,' Kate began tremulously, and the dark brows shot up in arrogant surprise.

'*Dios!* She is impossible. I have known about her for longer than she imagines. *There* is a young lady who wishes to acquire wealth the easy way, with no work involved. She attached herself to Javier and, as she too lives for the bright lights and the casino, he was only too ready to be attached.'

'So you took her from him,' Kate murmured.

'It was the easiest way of going about things.' He turned to her fiercely. 'But I have never even kissed her. She was all too ready to agree when I invited her out. She had noted where the power and wealth was gathered, and, though she set my teeth on edge, Javier was safely out of her clutches.'

'You greeted her lovingly when we came back from the beach,' Kate protested fiercely.

'I spoke to her softly,' he corrected. 'You were there, and I wished to give the impression that she was important to me.'

'You succeeded,' Kate complained, but he laughed and pulled her to him, cradling her head against his chest.

'I needed a refuge. I was not then sure that you would have me, and after kissing you in the cave I was walking on very thin ice.'

Kate relaxed as he rocked her in his arms, and then she found the courage to ask the question that had lingered in her mind for so long.

'Why did you send us away when we came to the *monasterio*?' she whispered, even now afraid of his answer. 'You knew that it was Javier who was forcing his attentions on me, but you blamed me and made us go.'

'Don't!' he groaned. 'Do not torture me, Kate. Do you imagine I have not tortured myself often enough when *Abuela* looked at her photographs and sighed over Lucia?'

'She agreed to our going. I asked her,' Kate confessed shakily, distressed to see torment on his face.

He turned to face her, his hands stroking her hair, his eyes moving over the bright and glorious colour. 'You were seventeen,' he reminded her. 'You came like a bright star to the quiet of the *monasterio*. Your eyes were like blue velvet, your hair a blaze of fire. You were enchanting, slender and graceful, eager and alive. I was twenty-eight and I found myself falling in love with a girl who was only just seventeen. I asked myself how long I would be content to merely look at you, and then there was Javier, who took you with him wherever he went and left me in an agony of fear for you. I know my brother well. When I caught him kissing you I knew you would have to go, for your sake and for mine. *Abuela* agreed. I do not think that she told Lucia.'

'And then you forgot all about me,' Kate said softly, her fingers trailing against his lips. He kissed them one at a time and looked at her seriously.

'There have been other women, *querida*. You were seventeen, and eight years is a long time. Very often I thought about you, wondering how you looked, how you would have changed, but I imagined that you would have

a settled life here in England. I had made up my mind
long ago that you were not for me. I had no such romantic thoughts as coming to find you when you were
old enough to marry me. It was over without even having
begun. You were a bright star that had passed through
my life.'

'I might never have seen you again,' Kate murmured
regretfully, and he hugged her close.

'When we received Lucia's letter my torment knew no
bounds. I had taken away *Abuela's* chance to be with
Lucia, and now it was too late. I hurried to England
hoping she would still be alive, but there was nobody
there and the neighbours told me you were at the church,
taking flowers.' His arms tightened. 'I saw you, your
bright hair blowing in the bitter wind, your slender
shoulders bowed, and I wanted to keep you close and
safe. When you turned, the same face that had haunted
my dreams looked blankly at me, the fire deadened, and
all the love surged back. This time I knew I would not
let you go.'

'Does *Abuela* know this time?' Kate asked hopefully,
and he smiled into her eyes.

'She does. I think she would have guessed anyway.
Those eyes miss very little. I told her that I loved you,
however, and she was happy. I was not so happy myself,'
he frowned. 'I was unsure about Merrol.'

'If I fluttered my eyelashes at him, he'd run a mile,'
Kate laughed.

'He would have to!' Diego said fiercely.

'What about my job?' Kate enquired worriedly, when
he had made her breathless with kisses, and he lifted
himself on one elbow, looking down at her.

'I have said that I would not keep you captive,' he
reminded her softly, 'but I could not live if you wished
to stay here in London. I have the family business to

run. It is a duty I cannot simply cast aside. I have thought about the problem and wondered how you would feel about working in Spain. Merrol wants to expand to there. Become the representative of Merrol and Jones in Spain. Become a partner. I will put up the money.'

'No fear!' Kate laughed. 'I'd love to do the work, but being a partner with Felix is taking things too far. Jones, whoever he was, died years ago. Felix owns the firm, and working for him is wonderful. Working *with* him would be a nightmare.'

'Then you agree to my suggestion?' Diego asked happily. 'You will work in Spain always?'

'Gladly.' She wound her arms around his neck. 'Felix wanted a toe-hold. That's me, until we have a family, and then I'll just go on and on making the *monasterio* more beautiful than ever. What about Javier?' she asked worriedly.

'Yes, Javier,' he frowned. 'I have spoilt him, and now he will take his fair share of the work. He can do the travelling when any long distance is involved, because I will not leave you for even one night. When he marries he will be too busy to chase the bright lights and the gaming tables.'

'Should you really force him to marry someone he doesn't care for?' Kate asked with a severe look at him.

'Doesn't care for?' He laughed down at her, his eyebrows raised in astonished amusement. 'You have not seen him with her! While you have been in Spain she has been in America with her parents. When she is back he is another person, following her like a lost puppy. He adores her.'

'Then why hasn't he married her already?' Kate asked in surprise.

'She is making him wait. She is a very sensible girl.'

'I see,' Kate murmured as he grinned down at her. 'I wonder what that makes me? Perhaps I should have taken the same line?'

His smile died and he cupped her face gently in his hands. 'You regret, my Kate?' he asked quietly, his dark eyes anxious.

'Oh, no! I love you, Diego. It's not in my nature to wait. I love you *now*, and I needed you now, just as you said I did. I'll always need you.'

She would. There was no other man in the world who could make her feel as Diego did, no other man who could storm into her heart and capture her.

'And I need you,' he confessed softly, his eyes gleaming with happiness. 'As you have a family in mind, we had better hurry home and be married in the white church in the valley.'

A wave of delight made her smile brilliant as she looked up at the man who hovered over her, his face possessive and tender. She didn't know how long the blossom would last—if it would still be there, a carpet of beauty to mark her passage to the lovely white church—but even if it had gone the memory would remain, and with it the knowledge that it would return each year to remind her.

'*Abuela* wouldn't be able to go there.' She suddenly realised that, even for this special day, Doña Elvira should not leave the *monasterio*.

'Then she will miss the ceremony,' he assured her steadily. 'She is aware of this. She will be able to attend the festivities in the great *sala* that you have restored so beautifully. It will be a fitting occasion for its opening. As to the ceremony, it requires only you and me. It will be our day—a day to remember always.'

She looked up at him with a glowing face, and he smiled, taking her into his arms.

'You see, I know you. I understand you. Even when we fight, deep inside we are one. I have captured you, *dulce amor mío*?' he asked against her lips.

'For always,' she whispered.

'And if I make love to you again now, you will not try to flee from me?'

'Would you let me?' Kate teased against his lips.

'Never, never, never!' he murmured as he drew her close.

She shivered with pleasure as his hands began to coax her, making her melt against him.

'I'll let Felix know about your great plan,' she sighed happily.

'But not now,' he murmured, as he closed her lips with his. 'The plan I have at this moment concerns only you and me, my adorable Kate.'

Celebrate the most romantic day of the year with
MY VALENTINE 1992—a sexy new collection of four
romantic stories written by our famous Temptation
authors:

> GINA WILKENS
> KRISTINE ROLOFSON
> JOANN ROSS
> VICKI LEWIS THOMPSON

My Valentine 1992—an exquisite escape into a romantic
and sensuous world.

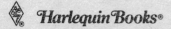 *Harlequin Books*®

HARLEQUIN *Temptation*

Rebels & Rogues

All men are not created equal. Some are rough around the edges. Tough-minded but tenderhearted. Incredibly sexy. The tempting fulfillment of every woman's fantasy.

When it's time to fight for what they believe in, to win that special woman, our Rebels and Rogues are heroes at heart.

Josh: He swore never to play the hero . . . unless the price was right.

THE PRIVATE EYE by Jayne Ann Krentz.
Temptation #377, January 1992.

Matt: A hard man to forget . . . and an even harder man not to love.

THE HOOD by Carin Rafferty.
Temptation #381, February 1992.

At Temptation, 1992 is the Year of Rebels and Rogues. Look for twelve exciting stories about bold and courageous men, one each month. Don't miss upcoming books from your favorite authors, including Candace Schuler, JoAnn Ross and Janice Kaiser.

Available wherever Harlequin books are sold. RR-1

Back by Popular Demand

A romantic tour of America through fifty favorite
Harlequin Presents, each set in a different state
researched by Janet and her husband, Bill. A journey
of a lifetime in one cherished collection.

In January, don't miss the exciting states featured in:

Title #23 **MINNESOTA**
            Giant of Mesabi

    #24 **MISSISSIPPI**
            A Tradition of Pride

Available wherever
Harlequin books are sold.

JD-JAN